Hittin' Licks For The Holidays

ATLANTA

ELIJAH R. FREEMAN

URBAN AINT DEAD

URBAN AINT DEAD PRESENTS

Hittin' Licks For The Holidays
Atlanta

By Elijah R. Freeman

URBAN AINT DEAD

Contact Author on FB: Elijah R. Freeman / IG: @the_future_of_urban_fiction

Contact Publisher at www.urbanaintdead.com

Email: urbanaintdead@gmail.com

ISBN: 979-8-9906748-7-5

SOUNDTRACKS

Scan the QR Code below to listen to the Soundtracks/Singles of some of your favorite U.A.D titles:

Don't have Spotify or Apple Music?
No Sweat!
Visit your choice streaming platform and search URBAN AINT DEAD.

Currently on lock serving a bid?
JPay, iHeartRadio, WHATEVER!
We got you covered.

Simply log into your facility's kiosk or tablet, go to music and
search URBAN AINT DEAD.

URBAN AINT DEAD

Like & Follow us on social media:

FB - URBAN AINT DEAD

IG: @urbanaintdead

Tik Tok - @urbanaintdead

SUBMISSIONS

Submit the first three chapters of your completed manuscript to <u>urbanaintdead@gmail.com</u>, subject line: Your book's title. The manuscript must be in a .doc file and sent as an attachment. The document should be in Times New Roman, double-spaced, and in size 12 font. Also, provide your synopsis and full contact information. If sending multiple submissions, they must each be in a separate email. Have a story but no way to submit it electronically? You can still submit to URBAN AINT DEAD. Send in the first three chapters, written or typed, of your completed manuscript to:

URBAN AINT DEAD
P.O Box 448
Maybrook, NY 12543

DO NOT send original manuscript. Must be a duplicate.
Provide your synopsis and a cover letter containing your full contact information.
Thanks for considering URBAN AINT DEAD.

Hittin' licks is my job. Do I like it? No, but it's the only way me and my little sister Jayla had been able to eat since my grandmother passed a little over two years ago. We have no other family—well...I don't. Ma Dukes died. She was an only child, and I never knew my dad. Jayla's dad was serving life in prison for killing a K-9 in a shootout with 12 during a drug raid. I was all she had, she was my world, and the reason I was on my sixth lick for today with four other niggas I didn't know from a can of paint the day after Thanksgiving.

"Yooo, Bam!" It was Quamain yelling from upstairs.

I walked into the kitchen to find Bam's short black ass eating raw peanut butter out a jar with a spoon. He'd raided the kitchen of every house we hit that day. We were the only two downstairs. Quamain, Bullethead and Noggin had been trying to get into the master bedroom for the better half of thirty minutes with no luck. I don't know what that was about, but I was ready to go.

"What's up, big bra?" Bam yelled.

"Go to the front room window and keep watch while we try to get in this room. We been in this bitch too long."

"Maaan." Bam made his way out the kitchen mumbling under his breath. He sucked his teeth. "Aiight, big bra."

I waited till Bam bent the corner before opening the refrigerator. I skipped breakfast this morning and was dehydrated. A bunch of aluminum foil covered leftovers from Thanksgiving, condiments, and a big jug of Sunny D. "Oh, hell yea." I grabbed it, popped the cap off and started to chug straight from the jug but thought better of it. For all I knew whoever lived here might prefer to drink from the jug, and just the thought of drinking behind a stranger made a nigga stomach turn. I walked to the counter and searched the wood cabinets above for a cup but there were only glasses, so I grabbed one.

"How we lookin' out there, Bam?" Quamain yelled from upstairs.

"Shiiid." I heard the blinds moving in the next room. "We good!" I poured a glass of Sunny D. "Aye, y'all!" Bam yelled.

I paused.

"What! W'sup?" Quamain and the others upstairs yelled in unison.

Bam was silent.

"Bam!" It was Bullethead this time. I could tell they were on edge, as I was myself.

"Shit, we good," Bam said. "A pickup truck pulled up outside, but they ain't pull in the driveway. Probably just live next door or something." I didn't realize I had stopped breathing until I resumed and began taking the glass of Sunny D to the head. "Oh, shit! It's an undercover!"

My heart stopped, the glass slipped from my fingers, and I was running before it shattered the floor behind me. Shooting straight out the backdoor, I was the first one out the house, racing toward the cut in the woods that we took to get here.

"Hey!"

I looked up as I passed the space that separated the house we hit and the house next to it to see a casually dressed thirty-something year old black man with a low cut running full speed at me with his gun aimed straight ahead. I tripped and fell just as the gun went off, and I dared not get back up. Fight or flight kicked in and I scrambled the rest of the way to the cut on all fours and stayed that way until I felt I was far enough in to get back right and run full speed ahead.

Gunshots rang out behind me, and I had to assume the man had opened fire on my accomplices. My heart was racing, and my head was spinning. Why was the police trying to kill us? I could hear sirens drawing near from three different directions, and despite the cool air and grey sky I was sweatin' like a mufucka as I tore through the woods like a crazed animal. Another shot rang out behind me, and the sirens seemed closer now.

I paused in the middle of the woods, out of breath, but all I could think about was Jayla at home alone waiting for me. I had to get off the scene and fast, but I didn't know which way to run. The sirens seemed to be coming from everywhere and that made me paranoid. There was a clearing to my right, and I ran to it in a frenzy. I reached the beginning of the clearing, which turned out to be someone's backyard in a row of houses in the same neighborhood as the house I just ran from.

There was a chain-link fence separating the woods from the backyard that I couldn't see before through all the trees, and I put my hands on top of it, hoisted myself up and swung my legs over, ripping my black basketball shorts as I came down on the other side. I ran through the backyard, hopped the fence again into the front yard, and was halfway through it when I caught sight of a red and a black Clayton County police squad car turning onto the street. I stopped abruptly with a little slide and ran back to the side of the house to duck off behind a big green Waste Management dumpster, hoping to God I hadn't been spotted. I peeked from the side as two squad cars shot by up the street, sirens blaring. Coast clear, I sprung from my hiding spot, crossed the front yard, and ran across the street into a cul-de-sac. A black woman who had been unloading groceries from her car in one of the driveways with the help of her kids saw me and panicked.

"Oh, my—" She dropped her bags and shielded her children as I passed by, hopping her neighbors fence into their backyard. I glanced back to see her rushing them in the house abandoning the food.

I faced forward and pushed on. Hopping another fence into another backyard, I ran along the side of the house and came out into another cul-de-sac where two guys, one light like me and one brown skin were standing on the block having a conversation beside a white Hyundai Elantra. I strode casually over to them deciding to try my luck. They looked street.

"Say, bra." They both stopped mid-conversation and looked back at me. "I can get a ride."

They looked me over from head to toe, taking in my sweaty disheveled look, the leaves and twigs I could only imagine we're in my dreads, my dirty used-to-be white wife beater, ripped basketball shorts and beat up black Air Force Ones that I wore whenever I put in work.

The brown skinned guy who I could see was at least forty now that I was closer was the first to speak. "Shiiid, it ain't my car." He looked the other way.

"Where you tryna go?" The light skin guy with long plaits spoke.

"Sierra Townhomes," I said. "On Godby."

He stared at me intently, and I looked him in his eyes as the blare of sirens became the plus one to my one that added up to two. "They lookin' for you?" I nodded. He looked back at the older guy, then back to me. "You kill anybody?"

I shook my head. "Nah. We broke in a house, and they shot at us. I don't know what the fuck goin' on. I just gotta get back to my little sister, bra. She alone right now and I'm all she got."

"We?!" Old School looked skeptical.

I ignored him and continued to look light skin head on.

He sighed. "Get in the back seat." I did just that, noticing for the first time a woman in the passenger seat. The guys on the block dapped each other up, then light skin hopped in the driver seat, crunk up the car, and pulled off.

"Who that?" Shawdy was a petite redbone who wore her hair in bangs. Couldn't have been too much older than me.

Light skin eased to a stop at the end of the street and made a left onto Helmer Road. Police cruisers flew toward us on the opposite side of the street, sirens blaring as the flashing red and blue lights danced on the roof. "Man, get down," Light skin said. "Sit on the floor. You hot as hell."

Again, I complied, and on the floor I remained. We reached the end of Helmer Road, made a right and I began to calm when we made it to Old National. I'd almost lost my life and freedom in the same day, and as we left Riverdale, riding into College Park it was all I could think about. The chances of either or happening was always a possibility in this lifestyle. I guess with Christmas being less than a month away the idea of Jayla spending it alone made it hit different. I rested the back of my head against the door and sighed with relief. I made it.

"I'm comin', Sis."

L ight skin dropped me off in the Old National Discount Mall parking lot and I walked the rest of the way to Sierra Townhomes in deep thought. After burglarizing six houses I was returning home empty handed and I ain't like that. All wasn't lost, though. I knew where everything was. Only thing about it was the guys I had hit the licks with wasn't my niggas.

They were Southside Fam, and I'd been turned onto them by my right-hand man, Tay. They had some moves, I needed some money, so I was down. We hit a lick in the Riverdale Trailer Park, two in Lake Ridge, then ducked everything off in a bando in Trinity Park before hitting three more licks on 1100 Block. I didn't know if any of them got shot or locked up today, but I knew if they got to the stash before I did, I wouldn't see a dime. The thought of being slimed out made me angry.

I hoped they wouldn't play the game raw like that, but I'd been in the streets long enough to know there was no honor amongst thieves. If it did go down like that, I had every intention of showing them I wasn't the average red nigga. The only thing that has ever been taken from me is my parents and my freedom. Jayla was my world and if I didn't provide for her, she would have gone without. I was no killer but taking food out of her mouth wasn't gonna be good for their health.

I took the back way instead of using the neighborhood entrance to avoid Ms. Paula at the front office. I was a week late on rent and I wasn't trying to hear her mouth. I got to the two-bedroom townhouse I shared with my baby sister and went around back. I never used the front door, and she knew not to answer it in my absence under any circumstances. I did the special knock that only we knew so she would know it was me and a few seconds later she peeked through the tall, white, hanging blinds and slid open the glass patio door. It was almost four in the afternoon, and she was still in pajamas with her long hair in a ponytail.

"You're home early." She stepped aside and I walked into the empty dining room, kitchen to my left. Short like my Ma Dukes, the top of Jayla's head barely reached the bottom of my chest, and I was 6'1. Unlike Ma Dukes, though, Jayla had a cocoa butter hue complexion.

Sliding the door shut behind me, I made my way to the downstairs bathroom passing the Loveseat and single couch living room along the way with Jayla on my heels.

"It didn't go well, huh?"

"Why you say that?" I cut the bathroom light on, walked to the sink, and twisted the knob to begin running water.

Jayla sighed. "Well, you don't look happy, for one. Then your clothes are dirty, ripped and you don't have anything."

I leaned over the sink, cupped my hands under the water and splashed it in my face. "I've come home empty handed on good days before."

"Yea, but you had money in your pocket." Jayla pointed at my shorts. "These ain't got none."

"Could be in my socks this time."

She rolled her eyes. "Whatever." I filled my hands with water and ran them through my dreads twice, then shook my head sprinkling water everywhere. "Ew!" Jayla threw her hands up to block her face. I laughed and tickled her sides while she was off guard with her hands raised. Her arms shot down instantly, and I moved my fingers about her body tickling her to the bathroom floor as we both laughed without a care in the world. Standing over her, I continued.

"Terrance!" Jayla giggled. "Terrance, stop!"

I tickled her some more. "You gone stop askin' questions?"

"Yes!"

"You promise?!" Tickle. Tickle.

"Okay, okay!" She wiggled about with laughter. It was her weakness. Jayla was extremely ticklish. "Wait! One more. One more! It's the last one for today. I promise."

I stopped. "One more what?"

"Question," she giggled.

My fingertips shot to her sides. "Is it about today?"

"No, no!" She shook her head, squirming to get from my grasp. "I swear!"

"Okay." I closed the lid on the toilet seat and sat down. "What is it?"

She sat up on the floor with her arms planted behind her and her legs straight ahead, toes up. "Are we behind on rent again?"

"No," I lied. "Why you—"

"Ms. Paula. She made her rounds this morning." Jayla's voice lowered and she dropped her gaze and began tapping her toes together shyly. "She came here twice, and she had that clipboard with her; the same one she had when she came to Traci's house that day we were over there buying food stamps. Traci told me she came over because she was a little behind. Said that's what those pink slips mean."

I stared at the top of her head shocked, but not really surprised. At ten years old, nothing got pass her. Jayla was smart, observant and didn't miss a beat. It was for this very reason that I was straight up with her about what I did in the streets for us to get by. I hit licks. That was my thing; and I made sure she knew that I would do that and whatever else I had to do for us to make it.

I wasn't playing with bands, but we wasn't just all the way fucked up, either. I may be late on rent from time to time but that was it. We both had new beds in our rooms, our cabinets and refrigerator stayed stocked with food and all of Jayla's favorite snacks and juices, and Jayla had about five or six pairs of Air Max 95's and clothes for days. I kept her clean and made sure she never went to school with anything less than five dollars in her pocket. If Mary McLeod Bethune Elementary was anything like it was when I went there, I knew the kids could be cruel. I refused to let poverty kill my sister's self-esteem.

So, what if I hit licks for a living? Who cares if I paid a couple junkies to steal the little furniture we had, and the flat screen television from Rent-A-Center? What difference did it make if I bought food stamps half price from the Section 8 hood rats around the way to make sure my sister could eat whenever she felt like it? I was eighteen and getting the job done.

"Jayla—"

"You don't have to lie to me, Terrance." She looked up at me. "Whatever's going on I know you got us."

We held each other gaze for a moment, and I sighed, dropped my head and nodded. "You right, Sis." I looked up. "Come here."

Jayla smiled and cocked her head at an angle. "You're not gonna hug me, are you?"

I laughed. "Girl, what is you talkin' bout?"

"You're dirty."

I laughed again. "Aiight, cool, cool. You got it. I won't hug you. Let me get in this shower 'fo you quarantine me."

"Right." She laughed and got up to leave.

"Jayla." I said just as she reached the door.

She paused and looked back. "Huh?"

"I never lied to you before. Ever. My bad for attemptin' to today. That was lame."

She nodded. "Okay."

"It won't happen again."

"I know." She turned around to exit the bathroom.

"Damn...say, Sis." I almost forgot.

She faced me. "Huh?"

"Christmas will be here before you know it." I stood up and looked under the sink for a bar of soap. "Made a list, yet?"

She shook her head. "No."

There was an *Irish Spring* pack, and I removed a bar from its contents. "Any idea what you want yet?"

"Uuuh." Jayla tilted her head up, looking at the ceiling for a moment before shrugging. "Nah."

I stared at her for a moment. "Well...think about it, okay?"

She smiled and nodded. "I will."

She walked out the bathroom, and I was stuck staring at the spot where she last stood, knowing by any means I would get her whatever was on her list, and wishing I could bring back the mother I knew she needed.

I stood outside, in the cold at the top of the neighborhood with Jayla at the bus stop aside from the rest of the kids. I was no longer worried about running into Ms. Paula. I had Traci take me to the bando the following morning after things went sideways and found everything in there just as we'd left it. A call to Tay and I learned among other things that no one was shot, but they had been arrested. I hit a few traps and got off the shit we struck for. I planned to shoot Tay some money for them after I pulled this move with D'narius this morning. Unlike a lot of these niggas out here, I didn't play the cross-out game. I knew better.

"You ain't cold?" Jayla asked, her breath visible as the

frost that covered the few cars that sat in the apartment parking lot.

"Nope! This hoodie is all I need." I reached down to fasten the top button of her coat. She wore that on top of a navy-blue polo shirt, khaki pants, and a pair of navy blue, tan and white Air Max 95's. I looked her in her eyes. "How you feelin'?"

"Good."

"Aiight, cool. That's what I like to hear." I pulled some money out my pocket, peeled off five dollars, and gave it to her as the bus rounded the corner headed our way from down of the street. "Oh, shit, there go the Twinkie. Time to be great." I kissed her cheek and stood. "You ready?"

"Yep!" Jayla was all smiles as she put the money in her pocket, pulling out a piece of paper in the same motion. "Here."

I grabbed it from her as the bus came to a stop and the neighborhood kids began to load up. I opened it. "Your Christmas list?"

She nodded. "If you can't get everything, I won't be mad. I know taking care of us isn't as easy as you try to make it seem sometimes. I put a star by things that are most impor-tant just in case."

I smiled. "You must want a wet willie in front of all yo lil' friends?" I licked my index finger.

"Okay, okay." She put her hands up in surrender.

"Don't worry bout me, young grasshopper. I am Mr. Miyagi of this shit. You are Daniel-san."

"You mean Jayla-son?"

"Girl, get on the bus!"

Jayla flashed her pearly whites and sprinted off to catch the bus. She got on, went to the back, and waved to me out the window. I waved back. The other parents began to walk off, but I stood posted, watching the golden yellow bus float down the street till it bent the corner. I pulled my Metro flip phone from my back pocket and checked the time. It was 7:36 a.m., which gave me eight hours to take care of business before I had to be back in this exact spot to get Jayla off the bus.

I already had the money order for my rent payment in an envelope, so I dropped it in the flap at the office and kept pushin'. I had a bus of my own to catch.

I HIT THE MARTA BUS STOP ON OLD NATIONAL AND RODE THE BUS to another stop up the street where I hopped off and made my way to Biscayne Apartments. I was here to link up with D'narius on a move he had in mind for us to get strapped. I walked through the neighborhood, which was unusually quiet, but I just chalked it up to how cold and early it was. I could still see my breath in the air. Zipping up my black hoodie, I stuffed my hands into the pocket and chuckled as I passed the green box that this nigga got robbed at while sitting a little over a year ago by a bitch name, Kush.

It was the talk of the Southside for at least six months after that. I heard about it before I saw it on YouTube, but when I did, I recognized her as the girl I stopped him from shooting at a party a couple days before she ran down on him. I respected her gangsta and as I knocked on an apartment door I wondered where she was. I stayed on the street she was from, but it had been at least two years since I'd seen her.

"Fool, I told you I don't want no damn wash towels!" I heard D'narius's muffled yell through the door before he opened it. "Aye, what's up, nigga!" He reached his hand out, and I dapped him up and entered his apartment.

This nigga was ugly as fuck. My skinny, brown skin partna with beady eyes and crusty lips who used to rock a low-cut Mohawk like Yung L.A...until Kush robbed him. Now, he had a plain-Jane even all around. Probably thought it would make him less recognizable.

"You watch too many movies," I said, recognizing the line from *Don't Be A Menace to South Central While Drinkin Yo Juice In The Hood.*

He laughed. "You know it."

His mama was sitting on the couch watching the news discuss the forecast for the week when I walked in. "Hey, Ms. Staci."

"Hey, Terrance," she said, dryly. She didn't so much as blink or look my way.

D'narius tapped my shoulder with the back of his hand. I looked at him, he nodded his head towards the stairs, and started them with me following close behind. We made a left at the top of the stairs and entered his room which was cluttered.

"Goddamn, nigga!" I ain't know what to do so I sat down on the edge of his twin size bed that sat straight across from the door, adjacent from his dresser that unfortunately was missing the drawers.

D'narius closed the door and looked around. "What?"

"Fuck you mean, what? Look at yo trap, shawdy." As if he couldn't see all the dirty clothes scattered about the empty room. Empty PS3 cases, unmade bed, and blunt ashes on his nightstand. I felt something under me and shifted raising my thigh so I could grab what turned out to be a copy of KING Magazine. "Let me find out you been beatin' yo meat in this dirty ass room."

"Of course I have. Everybody masturbates." He began picking up a pile of clothes and throwing them in the corner. "You're late. I told you we needed a car for this move."

"For what?"

"It's in Clay Co."

I sighed, shaking my head, and pinched the bridge of my nose. "Goddamn."

D'narius paused in the middle of the floor with a handful of clothes. "What?"

"I like to lost my freedom hittin' licks in Riverdale Friday." I watched a roach crawl across the top of the flat screen tv he had sitting on top of a kiddie table before disappearing inside. "Yea, man. A nigga hopped out shootin' at us, tryna dome somethin'. I wouldn't een be here right now if I hadn't tripped and fell while I was running."

"Naw."

"Yea and get this, the whole time I was thinking it was an undercover. Had me wondering why he was at us like that instead of tryna arrest us."

"Right." He agreed and tossed more clothes in the corner.

"Maaan, I talked to Tay who halla'd at bra them who I bussed the move wit'. You know they got caught. They say the shooter was the nigga who house it was."

"Damn." D'narius sat on the bed. "You straight?"

"Hell naw. Far from it actually." I faced him. "One or two things gotta happen, I either gotta find a less risky way to get money or I need to find some major moves so I ain't gotta be throwin' rocks at the chain gang everyday.

He nudged my knee with his fist. "And that's where I come in."

I stared at him for a few seconds. "Right."

"Naw, for real."

"I hear you." My voice dripped with sarcasm.

"Deadass. Look, I—" He paused and looked at the door.

"Hold on." Leaning over to his nightstand, he pressed play on the stereo and turned the volume up. "Lemonade" by Gucci Mane drowned us out. "Look, I already got us a whip to pull the move in. Peeled that mufucka this morning out somebody driveway off Pleasant Hill. I parked it in the parking lot up the block, so all we gotta do is ride out. Polo... these guns are it. Fuck kickin' doors! We layin' shit down. That's where the real money at."

D'narius slowed the stolen navy-blue Honda Civic as he came down Roundtree Road and made a left onto Hawthorne, entering a neighborhood filled with modest homes. This was a hood he frequented, and some guys he kicked it with had given him an inside scoop.

"That one." D'narius nodded at the cream-colored house, sitting on the corner of the block. We made a right, bypassing it as we rode up the street and parked in the driveway of an empty home. D'narius put the car in park, cut the engine, and faced me. "This a bando, we good. We won't be long anyways." He put one finger up. "Black .380," then another, "and a Russian K! That's all we came for. Let's be in and out."

He opened the driver's side door, and I followed suit. Telling me twice was something he didn't have to do. Not today. I didn't even ask questions. All I was thinking about as I crept through the backyards behind D'narius was Jayla's Christmas list. I had finally looked at it on the way over here, and it wasn't an outrageous list, but it wasn't cheap either. A digital camera, a Nintendo Wii, the latest T-Mobile Sidekick, some new Bratz dolls and accessories, another pair of Air Max 95s, and a bunch of clothes that I knew nothing about but was sure I could get Traci to point out for me.

I didn't know everything, but I knew she was getting everything on that list for Christmas. I'd make sure of it. Maybe because she deserved it, possibly because I loved her that much, or because deep down, I wanted to provide the Christmas a two-parent household could afford. I didn't want her to feel that loss, that sting of emptiness. It was a void that I needed and wanted to fill... so here I was.

"Polo!" D'narius snapped me out of my daze. "Goddamn, nigga! Stay with me!"

I shook it off. We were at the back of the house we were about hit. There was a wood porch on top of which sat a patio umbrella table. "I gotcha. W'sup?"

"I don't know." He was looking around. Catching sight of something, he walked over to a spot in the backyard close to the house. Reaching down, he picked up a rock the size of a baby fist. He walked back over to me. "This'll work."

He squatted down and looked under the porch, and I did

the same. The first thing I noticed was that it was dark and dirty, but then I saw the small windows aligning the house in a row sitting just above the ground. The house had a basement, and we would have to climb through the window and drop down into it.

I faced him. "You wanna bust the window with a rock?"

"Yeah." He nodded. "Just a light tap above where the latch is on the inside."

"Maaan, that shit gon' be loud as fuck."

"Not even. Ain't nobody finna hear this lil tinkle through the walls of their house. Not enough to pay attention. It's all in your head. Besides, people are still sleeping, anyway. It's nine o'clock in the morning." He stood, and I followed suit. He looked around again, eyes searching until they locked on the top deck of the porch. He pointed at the patio umbrella table. "Grab that umbrella and stick it at the bottom of the other side of the porch, and then turn it sideways so it can block us when we enter."

I did just that while D'narius climbed under the porch, and when I finished, I joined him. Inching closer to him, I noticed the heavy smell of raw earth underneath. It reminded me of afternoons toting Jayla on my shoulders and catching rollie pollies in my grandma's backyard. I smiled on the inside but remained pokerfaced. I had to stay focused.

D'narius cracked a small hole in the window above the latch, then reached in to unlock and open it. We climbed through and dropped down to the basement floor.

"I'll take downstairs, you search upstairs," D'narius instructed.

I nodded. "Bet!"

"Remember, we lookin' for a black .380 and a Russian K," he repeated what he'd said at his house earlier.

"Say less." I made my way upstairs and left him to do his thing. I wasn't worried about him getting down on me.

We had done this several times in the past to save time, and he always kept it real and cut me in. Even when he found valuables that we hadn't come lookin' for. He cut me in on moves that he did solo, and I did the same. D'narius wasn't the toughest nigga in the street, but I could trust him. Upstairs, I went sideways.

In every room, I searched closets thoroughly. I checked shoes, shoe boxes, shelves, and behind the doors. I searched every drawer in every dresser, shifted some shirts around in a top drawer, and found a small professional picture. There was a black and Puerto Rican guy with short, wavy hair and deep, black eyes, and a beautiful a yellow-bone chick with light brown almond eyes, full lips, and long, flowing black hair with streaks of Chestnut blonde. They were smiling. I could tell they were happy. Looked that way, anyway. I tossed it to the floor and continued searching the drawer.

I flipped mattresses, lifted pillows, looked under the bed, emptied the dirty clothes hamper, nothing! I flipped the bathroom and tore the kitchen up, looking for the straps, and still came up empty-handed. I couldn't believe it. This mufucka looked like the Tasmanian Devil had spun through this bitch and a nigga still couldn't find it. It had to be downstairs. That's the only thing that made sense to me, so I headed back downstairs to see if D'narius was having any luck.

I found him emptying the pantry on the house's main floor.

"Anything?"

He paused to look back at me. "Hell nah, you?"

"Hell nah."

"Damn!" He turned back around, frantic now, as he tossed dishware, spices, and pickled food to the floor. "They're here, bra! Somewhere in this house. I know they are!"

I watched D'narius carry on, and as bad as I wanted them to be here, I wasn't so sure anymore. I was curious as to what made him so confident the guns were in the house despite us having shaken this bitch down for the last twenty minutes and finding nothing. The thought of time set in, and I began to have flashbacks of the last lick I hit in Riverdale. We'd been in the house far too long. This shit was hot.

"Aye, man, we gotta dip." D'narius didn't deter in his search or respond. "Bra, we been in here too long. Let's dip, now!"

He looked back at me. "Bra, they in here. I'm tellin' you."

"Where they at then, bra?!" I threw my arms up.

D'narius looked defeated. "Man, fuck this shit. Come on."

We walked back to the basement window from which we'd entered. D'narius squatted and cupped his hands together for me to step on. I did so, and he stood, lifting me to the window seal. I grabbed it, pulled myself up, and went out the window. Outside, I turned around and reached in to pull D'narius up, but he was hesitant.

"D, w'sup?" I wiggled my fingers. "Come on, grab my hand." He looked back up at the door leading upstairs. "D!"

He shook his head. "Nah, man."

"Nah, man, what?"

"Take the car if you want." He tossed me the keys. "I ain't leavin' without that fye, bra."

"D!" I called out to him, but he was already sprinting towards the stairs.

"Fuck!" I looked behind me at the neighboring house, then I turned to let my eyes scan the houses that lined the side street.

I was officially paranoid. I had just been in a situation where a lick lasted too long and everyone who was involved outside of me was still locked up. That was just three days ago. I can't imagine what Jayla would do without me for twenty-four hours, let alone three whole days...or worse. My palms began to sweat despite the cool air and my eyes shot to the bottom of the stairs anxiously.

"D!" I whispered loudly. I heard a screen door open, and I

turned to see a middle aged black man with a low cut in office attire close and lock his door. "Shit!"

I looked at the time on my phone and it read 9:35. I looked to the bottom of the basement stairs, then back to the man who was now heading to his mailbox. Halfway there, he stopped and eyed the umbrella that kept us ducked off from one side curiously. I tensed up. My fight or flight senses were screaming for me to get out of there, but my street smarts were telling me not to move. If he looked flakey I could always take off, but I refused to leave D'narius behind unless I absolutely had to, no matter how wrong he was.

The guy scratched his head and shrugged. Walking the rest of the way to the mailbox, he opened it, pulled his mail from inside, and shuffled through the stack in his hand while walking to his car. I watched as he got in on the driver's side and backed out of the parking space a few moments later.

I glanced back and D'narius was runnin' back to the window. "I told you! Gimmie yo hands!" I laid flat and reached both of my hands in. He tucked something in his waist, grabbed both of my hands, and I pulled him up high enough to reach the window seal. He grabbed it, pulled himself up and out the window.

"I should beat yo ass!"

D'narius laughed and pulled the black .380 from his waist. "We ain't fightin' no more."

"Yeah, whatever, I'll still beat yo' ass."

He laughed again. "Man, quit cryin'. Come on, let's get from under this dirty ass porch and shoot back to the car."

D'narius drove and I sat in the passenger seat as we cruised up Bar Harbor Drive. It was a middle-class neighborhood in Lake Ridge with suburban homes, nicely trimmed lawns and tall wood fences that boxed in its occupants backyards. We slowed to a stop at a three-way and pulled curbside, outside a two-story corner home, on a hill to our right.

D'narius put the car in park and cut the engine. "Damn, I ain't been over this bitch in a minute." There was a burgundy SS Impala parked curbside in front of the house and a metal-lic, grayish blue Dodge Magnum.

"Yo!" D'narius went stiff. "Wh—who car that is?"

I followed his gaze to the burgundy SS Impala and

shrugged. "Shiiid, I don't know, nigga. Tay fuck wit a lil' some of everybody. You know he on wit' the weed now. Come on."

"Maaan...." D'narius didn't budge out his seat, nor did his eyes leave the Impala.

I opened the door, got out, and closed it behind me. I ain't know what his problem was.

As I walked to Tay's house, I heard D'narius' door open and close behind me. I reached the bottom of the porch and walked up to the rose wood stairs leading to the front door and knocked. D'narius came up the stairs behind me when Tay opened the door standing black and tall, bare chest with his dreads hanging over his shoulders.

"Sup, nigga?" Tay pulled his saggin' white shorts up over his boxers and dapped me up.

"What's up, foo? Wit' them long ass socks on." We bust out laughing.

Tay shrugged. "So. Shiiid, its cold as hell. Whaddup, D." Tay dapped D'narius up just as some guy with a light brown skin tone, and dreads that came to his chest came up behind him. He was medium height, with a medium build, and eyes that seemed to see right through you.

"I'm out, Tay." He looked at me and shifted his gaze to D'narius who was visibly shook.

Tay turned around and dapped him up. "Aiight, Redd."

Redd never took his eyes off D'narius, who now had his

eyes on the ground, shuffling his feet, nervously. Redd scoffed, smiled, and walked pass us.

"Free Kush," he let out as he walked down the steps.

"Fuck wrong wit' you?" I said to D'narius.

He looked up at me. "That's the nigga that recorded the bitch robbin' me in the hood."

Tay bust out laughing, and I looked across the yard at Redd who was still smiling, watching D'narius as he got in his car. I looked back at D'narius and shook my head. He could be a real bitch sometimes and that didn't sit right with me. There was no hoe in my blood. I wasn't going for nothing strange. I had a little sister to look after, and I needed niggas to know that I meant business.

My logic was, if they knew not to play with me, they would know damn well not to play with her. I had a couple niggas thought shit was sweet on the strength of me hanging with D'narius and they found out real quick that this wasn't that. So why did I still fuck with him, loyalty.

After my grandmother passed, my sister's aunty on her dad's side attempted to get custody of her, so I left Dill Avenue and fled to the Southside. I couldn't afford a spot at first, so I left Jayla to stay with my girlfriend at the time in Lakewood. D'narius was the first person I met out here. And when he found out all that I had going on, he started letting me crash at his place so I could save my money. Even after his mom's found out and kicked me out, he would sneak me in through the window late at night and I would sleep in his closet.

He'd even gone as far as to let me keep majority of the money from the licks we hit just so I could reach my goal faster. During this time, I'd enrolled my sister in home school. I'd go to Lakewood and spend the school day with Jayla and be ready and available for whatever D'narius had for us to get into to get some bread. It was a struggle getting from College Park to Lakewood everyday, but I wouldn't let a day go by where my sister didn't see my face. Eventually, D'narius would come through again and get a junkie from Hillandale named Charlie to agree to put my apartment in his name.

When the leasing office told Charlie he had to show proof that he made four times the monthly rent, D'narius got his mom's ex-boyfriend who owned a shipping company to make me some fake paystubs. I had only been sixteen at the time, new to the streets, and barely had resources. He came through for me. I will never forget that.

Tay's laughter slowed to a chuckle as Redd cranked up the car behind us and pulled off. "Man, come on..." Tay walked back in the house, and we stepped in behind him, into the foyer. To the left was a staircase leading upstairs and to the right, a separate stairway leading down. A little girl ran by upstairs while another little girl chased after her. Tay started downstairs but stopped when he heard a loud thud and the crashing of what sounded like a vase.

"Ania! Kia!" A female voice shouted. "Get in here and sit down somewhere!"

Tay shook his head as I closed the door behind us. "My mama finna be mad as hell." He continued on, and we followed him to his bedroom, which was directly to the right, at the bottom of the stairs.

Inside, straight ahead, sat his king-size bed. Directly to its left, pushed back against the wall, was a sofa; adjacent to it was a massive dark, cherry wood dresser. On top of it sat a 55-inch flat screen television. D'narius sat on the sofa, I flopped down on the bed, and Tay grabbed an iPod off a big, gray Panasonic television.

"Maaan, you still got that old ass TV." I pulled a bankroll from my pocket and counted out a few hundred.

Tay looked back down on the floor at it as if he didn't know what I was talking about without doing so. "Oh, shiiid, hell yea. This that mufucka. Everybody from Lake Ridge and just folks we all fuck with in general done signed it." He plugged the auxiliary cord into the phone and speakers and cut on "Southside" by Waka Flocka Flame.

"Roll somethin' up, Tay," D'narius said.

"What you got on it?" Tay turned around, and I handed him some money. "What's this for?"

"For yo people," I replied. "You know, for the licks, we hit in Lake Ridge before shit got crazy. It's for the stuff we ducked off before we hit 1100 Block. I split everything evenly."

"Damn..." Tay let out, surprised, while holding the money in his hand. "Niggas ain't keepin' it real like that no more. You the last of a dyin' breed, bra'."

I shrugged. "Just tryna steer clear of the other end of the stick, my nigga."

Tay's brow creased, and he cocked his head at an angle. "What?"

I laughed. "Nothin', bra."

He shrugged it off and turned to D'narius, who was now playing with a digital camera he had come across when he returned to the house. "Back to you. What you got on the weed? Tawmbout roll somethin' up."

"I got this." D'narius pulled the black .380 from his waist looking proud of himself.

Tay bust out laughing, once again at D'narius' expense. "This nigga had a gun and was still scared."

I watched all the bravado drain from D'narius' face and couldn't help myself this time. I, too, bust out laughing. He just knew he was going to get some cool points for being strapped, but it back fired. D'narius looked back and forth between me and Tay as we cracked up.

"Man, fuck both of y'all," he spat, putting the gun away. That only made us laugh harder.

"And, oh, so y'all strapped now, huh?" Tay questioned, turning around to his closet. He reached up on the top shelf and came down with a black .9 millimeter. He held it up, eyeing D'narius. "Yea, nigga."

D'narius sat up. "Where you get that?"

Tay pointed the gun at him. "Don't worry bout it, nigga!"

"Whoa!" D'narius put his hands up. "W'sup, bra, chill!"

I jumped up and put my hand on Tay's arm. "C'mon, Tay. You trippin'."

Tay smiled. "Haaa." He lowered his gun to his side, grabbed a sack of weed off the dresser and tossed it in D'narius' lap. "Roll that up." D'narius rolled up, Tay cut the music up, and we kicked shit. Tay fucked with D'narius, he just couldn't resist teasing him, especially after he let a girl rob him and ain't get no straightenin'. I mean, from what I've heard Kush was no ordinary girl, but still.

Hours passed and D'narius was out cold. I got to halla at Tay one on one and again he commended me on breaking Da Fam off and asked me about the comment I made about the other end of the stick. This time I explained to him what an O.G had taught me about social and natural laws, and consequences. While we are free to choose our actions, we are not free to choose the consequences of those actions. We can decide to step in front of a fast moving train but we don't get to decide what happens when that train hits us. We can decide to be dishonest in our business dealings, and while the social consequence may vary depending on whether or not we are found out, the natural consequences to our basic character are a fixed result.

I explained to him that our behavior is governed by principles. Living in harmony with them brings positive consequences, violating them brings negative consequences. We are free to choose our response in any situation, but in doing so, we choose the attending consequence.

"So, when we pick up one end of the stick, we pick up the other." I exhaled a heavy cloud of smoke and passed him the blunt.

He grabbed the blunt, held it, and smiled. "You look like a stick, ugly ass nigga."

We both laughed, high as hell.

"Shut the fuck up." My phone rang, and pulling it from my pocket, I looked at the screen and saw Traci's name pop up. I answered the call on the third ring.

"Hello?"

"We got a problem."

"Ma'am, could we have you step over here, please," I heard what sounded like 12 talk, followed by a call on a radio. I was all too familiar with the sound.

"Sir, could you give me a second? I'm on the phone with her brother now."

I sat up in alarm. "What's going on, Traci? Is Jayla okay?" Tay picked up on my shift in mood and sat still, watching my face in an attempt to piece together what was going on.

"Yeah, she's okay, but some lady was waiting at the bus stop and—." Before she could finish talking, she was cut off by the officer.

"Ma'am, I need you to hang up now and come talk to me so we can get this figured out." The phone disconnected after that, and I was on high alert. I had the slightest clue what was going on, but once I heard my sister and police, I knew I wasn't gonna sit around Tay's crib to try and put shit together. I had to see about my sister ASAP.

I was up and halfway out the door when I realized I didn't have a car. I cursed and rushed back down the stairs to wake D'narius, all while Tay yelled for me to tell him what was up. I heard myself scream that they were tryna take the only thing I had left as I shook D'narius forcefully. He fell off the couch and hopped up, alert. Tay stood back and watched the exchange.

"What the fuck?! What... what's going on?" Frantically, his beady eyes darted around the room, with confusion etched on his face.

I started to pace the floor. "They got her!"

"Who?"

"Jayla!" I shouted.

"Who got her?" D'narius adjusted the .380 in his waistband.

"Her auntie." I stopped in the middle of the floor, mid-pace, and faced him. "She got the police wit' her. We gotta get there, now! Let's go!" I turned around to shoot to the door.

"Bra, wait!" I turned back to D'narius to see what he needed me to wait for, after what I'd just told him. "We can't pull up in a hotbox with 12 on the scene," he said. "That'll only make a bad situation worse."

I threw my hands up. "Well, what do you exp—."

"Tiara will take you, bra," Tay said, cutting me off.

"Bet!"

TIARA DROVE THE MAGNUM DOWN OLD NATIONAL WHILE I SAT IN the passenger seat, hoping to God they were still there when we pulled up. It had been twenty minutes since I got the call from Traci. That twenty minutes felt like hours, and each passing second was slowly fucking me up inside. We made a left onto Godby Road and a right into Sierra Townhouses, and the first thing I saw was Jayla sitting in the passenger seat of her aunt's Toyota Camry. My eyes shifted, and I spotted Traci in the back of one of the two white College Park police squad cars. Jayla's aunt, Tabitha, stood outside of the car talking to one male and one female officer.

Tiara slowed to a stop in the middle of the street. "You want me to—."

I was out the door before she could put the car in park or finish her sentence. Seeing Traci in the back of a squad car made me livid. All that went through my head was, *what the fuck was she doing there.* I ran up on them, oblivious to the nosey onlookers throughout the townhouse parking lot.

"Yo, what the fuck is going on?" I questioned aggressively, stopping right outside of Traci's window. "Why the fuck is she in the back of the police car?"

Jayla's aunt raised her hand in an attempt to calm me down. "Terrance."

"Don't Terrance me!"

"She's not under arrest," the black female officer whose name tag read Harris said.

"So why the fuck is she—." Out of the corner of my eye, I saw Jayla waving her hand to get my attention. I turned enough to lock eyes with her, and she nodded twice and smiled. It was her way of letting me know she was okay. I took a deep breath and changed my approach. "So, why is she in the police car?"

"She refused to let the girl go with her aunt, her legal guardian," the black male officer explained. His name tag read Jackson. "When we arrived at the scene, she was unruly, so we placed her in the back of the squad car until she calmed down."

"Aiight, cool." I looked through the window at her. "You

calm?" Traci nodded. "Bet." I slapped the roof of the car twice. "She's calm, let her out."

The officers looked at each other and then at Tabitha.

She shrugged. "Let her out."

The female officer opened the door, and by the mug on her face, I knew Traci wanted to say something smart, but she held it down.

"You good?" I touched her arm.

Staring a hole through Tabitha, she nodded. "I'm fine."

"Cool." I turned to Tabitha and nodded toward her car, where Jayla was still seated, staring in our direction. "Okay, her next."

Tabitha sighed. "I'm afraid I can't do that, Terrance, and you know it."

I narrowed my eyes and took a step closer to her. "Fuck you mean you're afraid you can't?"

Officer Jackson stepped halfway between us. "The girl will be leaving with Ms. Henderson, as she is her legal guardian."

My face screwed up, and I snapped. "That's bullshit!"

"Terrance—" Tabitha started.

"Ain't no mufuckin' Terrance! I'm eighteen now." I looked her up and down, my frustration mounting with each passing second. "I'm her legal guardian!" The officer looked back and forth between us, likely trying to figure out who was telling the truth.

"I am Jayla's legal guardian, Terrance," Tabitha stated

calmly. Her eyes begged me to be peaceful, but I was anything but that. And quite frankly, she had me fucked up.

"How? We never went to court for this to be legal." I pointed to Tabitha's car towards Jayla whose eyes held confusion. I knew she was trying to put things together by our body language. "Ask her who she wants to stay with."

"While the child does have a say in the matter, it is an issue that would have to be resolved in court." Officer Harris spoke for the first time, and he, too, was saying some bullshit I didn't wanna hear. "But, right now, as it stands, she—."

"I am Jayla's legal guardian, Terrance," Tabitha stated, cutting Officer Harris off mid-sentence. "My brother signed his rights over to me after you disappeared with Jayla, without a word, might I add. I gave you time with her because I understood that a lot was going on at the time with your grandmother passing and she was all you had. You could've just come to me, and we could've figured this all out, but you took her instead. I have been beyond patient with you."

"Took her?" I sucked my teeth. "My sister wants to be with me. I did what I was supposed to because I'm all she has and the most consistent thing in her life."

Tabitha held her hand up, palm forward, signaling me to stop talking. "While that may be the case, she has other family, and what you did was wrong. I only want what's best for her."

"And what you think I want, huh?" The fact that we were

still out in the open having this conversation further added to my level of frustration. And in a minute, I was going to say fuck Tabitha being Jayla's aunt, and just go ham on her ass.

Tabitha paused and looked me in the eyes. "I honestly think you want the same thing, Terrance, but look around you," she waved her arm about the neighborhood, "this ain't it."

A group of women who looked about Tabitha's age, who had been watching from the sidelines, shook their heads and walked off. "Bitch," one of them mumbled under their breath.

Tabitha's eyes cut their way back to me. "I didn't say that to be insulting, but you have to admit this isn't the best environment for her." She pointed at a building just to our right. "Bullet-ridden buildings, Terrance? No."

"I got her. She straight."

"But who's gonna watch over her while you work? Do you even—." She glanced over at Officer Jackson. "Never mind."

"I watch her while he's at work," Traci said. "I was here to get her when you showed up."

"And I work at the chicken plant as a forklift operator. This environment," I made the same gesture around the neighborhood as she had done, "is only temporary."

Tabitha's eyes shifted between Traci and me, and though they said we were full of shit, she didn't voice it. "Well, however true all of that may be, the courts have granted me full custody. I don't mind you seeing Jayla and spending time with her at my place. You're always welcome. As far as me allowing you to leave with her, I'm not sure I'm comfortable with that. All and all, it's for the best. I truly hope you understand that."

"Yeah, I understand." I nodded.

Tabitha closed her eyes and sighed. "Thank y—"

"I understand that you on some bullshit."

"Terrance," she said.

"It's all good." I walked away from her, went to the passenger side of her car, where Jayla sat, and opened the door.

"About time!" Jayla let out while stepping out of the car.

I glanced back at Tabitha and the police, mugging them hard and gritting my teeth. Turning back to Jayla, I softened my expression and kneeled in front of her. "Hey, umm..."

Her brow creased, and she cocked her head at an angle. "What, what's wrong?"

I shook my head and gave a weak smile. "Nothing. You just... you're gonna have to go away for a lil' while that's all, but—"

"What?"

I swallowed the lump in my throat. "You're just goin' with your aunty for a lil while. Nothin' permanent, just until—"

"But I don't wanna go with her. I wanna stay with you and Traci."

I nodded. "I know."

Jayla's eyes welled up with tears. "Did I put too much on my Christmas list?"

"Of course not, Lala. Come on, now."

"Well, what is it? Why do I have to go?" One lone tear cascaded down her soft, brown cheeks, and my whole world shattered.

My will to be strong for her was the only thing keeping me together. "Because a judge said you have to, and the police are going to see to it that you do, but—"

"No!" Jayla shook her head. "I'm not going!"

"Jayla." Tabitha came up from behind me and was now reaching for Jayla.

She snatched back from her reach. "No! I'm staying with Terrance!"

Hearing Jayla shouting, the officers had walked over and were getting a little too close for me. Officer Jackson approached first, leaning down a little, he spoke to Jayla.

"Jayla, is it?"

"Aye, man, back the fuck up!"

Traci rushed over to me and grabbed my arm. She knew I didn't play when it came to my sister. This shit would turn into an assault on a police officer charge real quick.

Officer Jackson raised his hands. "I'm just tryna help," he reasoned.

"Well, help y'all ass over there, shawdy." I pointed to

their squad car. "Y'all trippin'. She don't need y'all surrounding her."

"Aye, who do you think you talkin' to? You better show some goddamn—."

I lost it. "Nigga, you, nigga!"

"Oh, you think you tough?" He went to unbuckle his duty belt.

"What's up!" I advanced towards him while Traci struggled to hold me back.

"Terrance, you're not thinkin'," she said. "Terrance!"

"Nah, I'm finna show him." I pulled my pants up. "Take that badge off, bitch ass nigga."

Jayla was boo-hoo crying now, and that made me even madder. Looking past the officer, I could see that Tiara had gotten out of her car and was standing beside it. Tabitha stepped in between me and the officer and used her arms to create space between us.

"Look, Terrance, you're upset, but think about your future."

"Nah, fuck that!"

Officer Harris slid behind her partner and whispered in his ear, patting him twice lightly on the shoulder. Jackson relaxed visibly and refastened his belt.

"Talk to your sister, man." Now, his bitch ass wanted to be encouraging. I watched as they walked back towards their squad cars.

Tabitha and Traci seemed to relax. I turned around, took

a knee in front of Jayla, and placed both hands on either side of her shoulders. She was sniveling and visibly shook.

"Listen, Lala. I need you to be strong for me, okay?" I looked her dead in her eyes. "You trust yo brother?" She nodded and wiped her eyes. "Have I ever lied to you?" She shook her head. "Okay, then," I said. "This is only temporary. I'm coming to get you, you hear me?"

She nodded her understanding. "Uh-huh."

"Aiight now, gimmie a hug and stop crying."

We hugged for a moment that I wanted to last forever, but if it did I wouldn't be able to keep my promise. Nothing in this world would stop me from doing that. If there were anyone she would always be able to count on, it was me. I released her from my embrace and she climbed back into the car, this time with Tabitha getting in the driver's seat. I watched the car back out, pull off, and exit the townhouses with one thing on my mind: turning this situation into motivation to fight harder for her return.

I awoke the next morning feeling emptier than the townhouse I rested my head. I had my curtains drawn, making the room pitch black, which unfortunately matched my mood. I hadn't been right mentally since Jayla was taken away from me, and I didn't think I would be until I got her back. She had become my sole purpose. My drive for everything I did, my motivation to want better and to be better. For the last two years, it had just been us, and like that, she was gone.

I looked over at my nightstand at the red numbers on my digital clock. It was 9 o'clock on the dot, which meant I'd only gotten four hours of rest. Sleep had been hard to come by. Every time I closed my eyes, I saw Jayla's tear-streaked face. The image was embedded in my memory.

Sitting up, I brought my legs over onto the floor and sat on the edge of my bed in my boxers. Placing both hands on my head, I leaned forward, resting my elbows on my knees. I had to figure something out. I had been racking my brain about where to start, but all of this was new to me. Never had I been in a situation where I had to play by the rules of any system. I had always done things my way and got by, which is the main reason why I played it the way I had when I saw this shit coming the first time.

At sixteen, I'd just lost my grandma, who was the only thing keeping me and Jayla together. Tabitha worked the night shift at the airport and stayed with us when she got off, until the funeral. Then, that night, after we laid my grandmother to rest, Tabitha came to my room before she left for work. I was deep in my thoughts, flipping through the family photo album when she knocked.

"Knock, knock..." I turned to see her in my doorway, with her airport personnel uniform on and her clearance card around her neck. "Can I come in for a sec?"

I turned back and continued flipping through the pages. "Sure."

"What you doing?" She asked, walking in and sitting beside me. "Going through your grandmother's old photo album, I see."

I flipped to the next page without a word.

"You okay?"

"Yeah." I kept flipping pages. I wasn't trying to be rude. I was still numb from the loss and didn't feel like talking.

"Okay...so," she cleared her throat, "I'll be taking custody of Jayla soon."

I glanced up at her and back down to the photo album. I paused on a picture of my grandmother in her younger years and stared at it. "Okay," I responded dryly.

"Only Jayla."

My eyes met hers again, and with a straight face, we locked eyes and held each other's gaze for a moment, letting the reality of her words hang in the air. "Okay." I looked back down at my grandma and flipped the page.

"You don't... would you like to know why?"

I shrugged. "It is what it is."

I could feel her eyes burning a hole in the side of my face as a pregnant pause passed between us. "I just don't think I can take care of you both. Not that I don't want to, its just— I can't afford to, right now. Not to mention Collins. He doesn't like the idea of you mov—."

"I said, it is what it is." I closed the photo album and looked up at her with a straight face.

Tabitha lowered her gaze, dropped her head, and nervously rubbed her hands down her pants legs before standing. "Right. So, I'm gonna head to work now."

"Aiight." I refocused on the photo album in my lap as she quietly exited my room. When I heard the front door open and close, I launched the photo album at the lamp on my nightstand, shattering it completely. Breathing heavily, I balled my fist up and gritted my teeth.

"What's wrong, Terrance?" I turned to find Jayla standing in my doorway, rubbing her eyes with the back of her hand in her Tinkerbell pajamas.

Instantly, my expression softened. Jayla was my kryptonite. "Nothing, Lala. I'm aiight."

She pointed to my shattered lamp. "What happened to your light?"

"I broke it on accident." I waved her over. "Come here. Did I wake you up?"

"Yes," she said, walking over to me.

I picked her up and sat her on my lap. "I'm sorry. You know I can be clumsy sometimes." I made a silly face, and she laughed, reminding me of Ma Dukes. I couldn't help but smile. "You laugh like mommy."

"I know, Terrance. You only tell me everytime I laugh." Jayla rolled her eyes.

I busted out laughing. "Don't roll yo eyes at me. You do! And where you learn to roll your eyes? Who taught you that?"

Jayla sighed. "Was mommy fun?"

"Super fun. Like a younger version of grandma...before grandma got sick." I bit the inside of my lip, feeling the sadness creeping back in.

"Terrance, are we all we got now?"

I looked at her, brows creasing in curiosity. "Huh?"

"Before grandma got sick, she told me that one day she wouldn't be with us because she was getting old. She told me not to be sad because she was going to God's Kingdom, and she

would be waiting for us, but we would have each other. She told me that the only person who loved me more than her was you and always to trust you because once she was gone, we were all we got."

For a moment I said nothing, then I pulled her into my embrace and hugged her tight. My grandma had found a way to speak to me beyond the grave, and in my mind, at that moment, I was hugging both her and Jayla. I shed a tear behind Jayla's back but quickly wiped it away before pulling back and tapping Jayla's leg.

"Get dressed and pack a suitcase. We outta here."

She looked up into my eyes. "We're leaving?"

"Yeah." I nodded.

She held my gaze, searching my soul. "We're not coming back, are we?"

I shook my head. "No."

"What about Auntie Tabby?"

I sighed. "She's the reason we gotta go."

"Why?"

"She wants to take you away from me."

"But why?"

"I wish I knew, but I don't, Lala. I can't let them separate us, though. So, come on." I tapped her leg, she hopped up, and I stood. "Go get ready. Pack as much as you can and take whatever you want. I'll figure out the rest."

"Okay." Without further questioning, Jayla hurried out of my room and back to hers to get dressed and pack. I did the same, and

in less than an hour, we were saying bye to our grandma's house
for the last time.

Now, looking back, I have no regrets. They had me fucked up then like they got me fucked up now. I just wanted to do it the right way this time. I had to ensure that Jayla would never experience anything like this again. I don't think her life thus far would be considered normal by anyone's standard, but I wanted it to improve.

There was a knock at the front door, and I got up and put on a wife beater and pair of basketball shorts before answering it. I looked through the peephole and saw Traci at my doorstep. She was dressed casually in a fitted grey hoodie, light-washed skinny jeans that hugged her thick-petite frame, and medium chestnut Ugg boots holding a Styrofoam tray covered with aluminum. I unlocked the door and opened it.

"Hey." She smiled; shiny golden bronze skin glowing.

"W'sup."

She held up the plate. "Brought you something to eat. I figured that with everything going on, the last thing on your mind would be feeding yourself. I can't have you out here wasting away."

"Oh, 'preciate it." I grabbed the plate from her and sniffed it. "Hell, you done burnt up tryna feed me?"

Taking a step back, she sucked her teeth and scrunched her face. "Boy, don't do me."

I smirked. "Nah, I'm bullshittin'. Tryna step in right fast?"

Traci smiled and shrugged. "Sure, I guess I got a minute."

I stepped aside, she walked in, and I smiled, looking down at her. She wore her hair in micros and was just short enough for me to see over her head. I closed the door once she was inside. "You thirsty?" I headed to the kitchen.

She was right behind me. "Depends on what you got to drink."

"Well." I stepped into the kitchen and opened the refrigerator. "Thanks to you and Jayla, we got damn near every juice you can think of." I took a deep breath and exhaled. It hurt to say her name, knowing she wasn't here with me.

"Juice is fine," Traci said.

"Bet." I grabbed the apple juice from the refrigerator and closed the door. Turning around, I reached up into the pale white painted cabinets and grabbed a cup.

"Sorry about yesterday." I sat the cup on the counter and unscrewed the top of the jug of apple juice.

"Nothing to be sorry about, wasn't your fault. Shiid, you damn near went to jail for lil sis. I appreciate you if anything."

"Oh, you know I wasn't going for nothing strange. I'm like bitch, who is you?!" She laughed as she watched me pour her drink. I handed her the cup.

"Any idea how you gone go about getting her back?" Traci

took a sip of her drink and cleared her throat. "Whew! I did not know my throat was that dry." She laughed, and I smiled, though my mind was a mile away from the kitchen. I was present physically, but mentally, I was with Jayla. "I googled some stuff regarding custody rights and things that could better your chances as far as what judges look for and having a stable household is top of the list. I could get you a job working with my uncle's landscaping company, and if you needed me to lie on your behalf and say we live together, I'd be down."

I looked at her, then down at the floor in deep thought. Putting my back up against the counter, I took a deep breath. Exhaling, I pinched the bridge of my nose and squeezed my eyes tight. "I couldn't ask you to do that, Traci. It sounds good, but I doubt it would be that simple. I'm sure they would want you to show proof of residence. You would have to move in for real. Then you'd lose yo food stamps."

"You know that doesn't matter to me." We locked eyes, and she held my gaze. "I just wanna make sure y'all good; that's all I care about. We've become close in the last two years, and I know what Jayla means to you and what she's come to mean to me."

I opened my mouth to respond, and my phone rang in my shorts pocket. "Hold n, one sec."

"Do you," Traci said, taking another sip of apple juice.

Pulling my phone from my pocket, I looked at the screen to see Tay calling. I pressed the green call button and answered the phone.

"Bro!

"W'sup, man. You aight?"

"Yea, maaan. I'm good for now. I'm tryna figure out the best way to get sis back. May need to hire a civil lawyer to fight this shit." Sighing, I shook my head and rubbed my temples. "I ain't een got no fuckin' money." Traci watched me, listening to my unilateral conversation.

"That's what I'm callin' you for," Tay said. "Tiara told me what happened yesterday. Shit fucked up. I been hearing you loud and clear in our conversations. D'narius also mentioned what you told him about you either needing to find a less risky way to get money or find some major moves, so seen gotta be throwin' rocks at the chain gang every day."

"Yea, and?"

"I think I got just the move you lookin' for."

CHAPTER 8

"Goddamn, it's cold in this mufucka. Cut the heat on."

"Can't," Tay said, flipping the light switch up and cutting the lights on as we walked into his bedroom. "The gas off."

"Oh, hell naw. Y'all trippin'. It's winter." I sat on the edge of the bed. "Where the hell D'narius go? I thought you said he was still over here. I coulda told ol' girl to wait for me if he wasn't."

Tay sucked his teeth. "Maaan, he just left!" He went to his dresser, reached in a rectangular box and removed a Swisher Sweet cigarillo. "He got a call from somebody, got up lookin' all serious and alarmed and shit. I asked him what was up, but he shot up out of here. Ain't say shit. Scary ass..."

Tay grabbed a small trash can from the side of the dresser, came over and sat on the bed beside me, sitting the trash can on the floor in front of him. He bussed the cigarillo down the middle, dumped the guts in the trash, pulled out a sack of weed and began breaking it down into the swisher. As I watched him roll, I wasn't sure what to make of D'narius' behavior, but I had my own problems at the moment. Making a mental note to check on him later, I put my mind on the reason for my visit.

"So, what's up, though," I asked.

"I got a move." Tay was locked in on the blunt, tucking and rolling the weed into the cigarillo.

I let his statement hang in the air for a minute before getting impatient. "And?!"

"It's major."

"Okay, so what the fuck is it?"

Tay shrugged. "Now, that's what I don't know."

"So, how you know it's major if you don't een know what the play is?"

"The guy who brought it to me." Tay began licking the blunt, sealing the weed inside. "He bout his business and he told me so. You think I'd be playin' wit you at a time like this, knowing what's at stake?" Tay brushed weed residue off his lap, and began patting his pockets in search of something, before looking to me. "You got a lighter on you?"

"Fasho." I reached in my pocket, removed my black BIC lighter and handed it to him. "So, who the nigga is?"

"Redd."

"Who?"

Tay lit the blunt, took a deep pull, and exhaled a cloud of smoke, coughing. "Redd. Bra, wit' the dreads who was leavin' when you pulled up yesterday."

I thought back to yesterday afternoon. "The nigga that got beef wit' D'narius?"

Tay sucked his teeth. "Man, ain't nobody got beef wit' that scary ass nigga. He just a bitch that— and I know this ya homeboy, but you know it's true— he just a bitch that tried to pump his nuts up on the wrong broad and got put back in his place." Tay hit the blunt. "I don't know if you know her, but uuh..." he exhaled a cloud of smoke. "...the bitch is gangsta."

"Who?"

"Kush."

Tay passed me the blunt and I accepted, put it to my lips and pulled, thinking back to the caramel skin toned girl with the jet-black hair and green eyes. That was the first and last time I ever saw her.

I exhaled. "I know of her, but I don't know her."

"Yea. Well, anyways...Redd. He got a 20k play, but he said if he told me he'd have to kill me."

I looked at him, and we bussed out laughing.

"I'm bullshittin' but I'm not. He really said that."

I stopped laughing, and my brows creased in suspicion. "You think he dead ass?"

"Shiiid, nigga I don't know. Pass the blunt."

"Oh, damn." I passed him the blunt and watched him take a hit. "Sooo—."

"All I can tell you is this." Tay blew out a cloud of smoke. "He ain't known for makin' idle threats and he most definitely bout his paper. That in mind, I wasn't tryna find out. But if you need that lawyer money, there it is." He took a long pull from the blunt and exhaled. "Just make sure you down for whatever."

Tay made the call to Redd, who shot him an eastside address off McAfee Road for us to meet him later on that night around 9 pm. I hated the idea of waiting that long. The thought of being idle while Jayla waited for me to come get her was unbearable.

"What's worse," Tay said, "being patient and waiting till 9 to meet Redd, or being thirsty and catchin' an unnecessary case before 9? Then you really gon' have to wait. Choice patience is better than forced patience any day, my nigga."

I nodded. He was dead ass right. The last thing I wanted to do was make a bad situation worse, so there I waited. From sitting at the edge of Tay's bed, back and forth to the door helping him with plays, raiding the kitchen refrigerator, to kickin' back on the couch in his room, I waited.

An hour and a half before meeting Redd, Traci texted me some Georgia child custody case lawyer info. Their average retainer fee was between $3000 to $5000.

Me: Thanks, Traci.

Traci: You're welcome. Anything else I can do just let me know.

Me: 4sho.

I fucked with Traci. Shawdy was a real one, fasho. Since day one, she had been a big help with Jayla, and over time they had developed a big sis-lil-sis type of bond to where now Traci had damn near gone to jail to make sure she was good. I hadn't let on as much, but that whole incident had me looking at her a little differently. Then after our talk this morning with the info she'd looked up on our behalf and her willingness to move in with us to make our story believable... I don't know. Loyalty has always been an attractive trait in women for me. And although Traci was physically fine, I had honestly never looked at her that way.

But lately...

A knock at the front door snapped me out of my thoughts. Seeing Tay on his cell phone, fixing up some sacks at the digital scale on top of his dresser, I got up and headed upstairs. I got to the door, opened it, and was surprised to see D'narius standing on the porch with some light-skinned guy with short, wavy hair. He was on his phone. I looked at D'narius, who stood slightly behind the guy's left shoulder, eyes full of terror. Frantically, he mouthed something to me that I couldn't make out. I shifted my gaze back to the light-skinned guy.

Something about him looked familiar, but I knew I had never met him before. He hung up and looked at me with those deep, black eyes, and instantly, I knew exactly where I knew him from. I couldn't believe my eyes. It was the Black and Puerto Rican guy from the picture with the light brown skin girl that I found in the drawer on the lick we hit earlier.

"Go get my camera," he said, his voice hoarse and sinister.

"What?!" I sounded more aggressive than I meant to, but I was hot that he was even here. This could only mean one thing. My eyes shot to D'narius and if looks could kill.

"I said, go get my camera."

Tay came up from behind me and opened the door a little wider. "I told you I—." He stopped mid-sentence, looked at me, then back at the light-skinned stranger on his porch. "W'sup?"

"My name Miami Phat. All I want is my camera." He pointed back at D'narius. "He told me I could find it here."

I snapped. "Look, we ain't got shit for you homes!"

He focused his attention back on me and narrowed his eyes. D'narius was shaking his head in urgency behind him, but I could care less. I couldn't believe this man!

The guy dialed a number and put the phone to his ear. "Bring the whole arsenal!"

"Man, nigga I—."

"Chill," Tay said, cutting me off. Turning to Miami Phat, he held up a finger. "Hold on, brah. Pause."

"One sec," he said into the phone. He looked at Tay. "I just want my camera."

Tay pushed the door up till it was all but closed and turned to me. "Brah, you might as well give that man his stuff back."

"Maaan, fuck no! I ain't givin' that nigga shit. They strapped, we strapped. You know how that shit go."

Tay sucked his teeth. "Polo, man, we got one gun in here. This nigga on the phone tawmbout, bring the whole arsenal. I got my sister and her kids upstairs, we still gotta get up with Redd in a hour. We really need to be on the road now. Ween got time for this. Let him have it."

As much as I hated to admit it, he was right again. The sounds of his nieces giggling upstairs further drove home his point. I went downstairs, grabbed the camera, and felt conflicted inside on my way back up. I was raised in the streets not to give shit back that you took, but it is what it is. Jayla was more important. Besides, it was my fault for hittin' licks with D'narius, knowing he wasn't cut like that anyways. I had to take accountability, but I was still mad.

Tay moved to the side, and I opened the door, holding the camera out to Miami Phat. "Huh, get 'cha shit."

Miami Phat stared at me for three heart beats before grabbing the camera. He turned to D'narius. "Let's go." Like the bitch he was, D'narius turned and walked down the porch steps. Miami Phat brought the phone to his ear once more. "Stand down." He ended the call, put his phone in his pocket, then looked from Tay to me. "You talk too much."

We stood there having a standoff until Miami Phat turned and walked down the porch steps. Behind him, D'narius had just made it to the passenger door of the white Chevy Malibu parked in front of the house.

I slammed the door. "That nigga D a hoe!"

Tay shook his head. "That's ya, boy."

Again, I found myself riding in the Dodge Magnum, with Tay as the driver. We were cruising through the light traffic on I-20 on our way to the Eastside to meet up with Redd. It wasn't long before we were pulling curbside, behind an all-white van, in front of a white house, beside which was a driveway that led a little pass the house to a two car garage that sat separately. There were two dark-colored cars in the driveway, but it was hard to make out the models due to it being nighttime. Tay cut the engine.

"Who spot this is?" I was looking at the house's windows half expecting to catch someone peeking out.

"This One-Way spot," Tay said. "The hood pawn shop."

I looked at Tay.

"Deadass. He don't rob, trap or none of that. He buy low and sell high. So, now that you've been invited out here by Redd, you good." Tay adjusted the rearview mirror and pulled out his phone. I'm texting him now to let him know we out here, but yeah. You know Redd originally from the Eastside. This one of his resources. Anytime you hit a lick, you can bring it straight here. You ain't gotta sit on nothing. One-way'll buy it all, no matter what, as long as it can be sold. Straps, flat screens, laptops, electric scooters, whatever! His motto is— Hold up, that's Redd right there." With the back of his hand, Tay tapped my shoulder twice. "Come on, let's go."

We got out of the car and met Redd halfway in the middle of the yard.

"W'sup, Redd," Tay said.

Redd embraced Tay in a handshake hug. "W'sup."

Tay released him, stepped back, and pointed to me. "This my boy, Polo, who I was tellin' you bout."

Redd tossed his head back in the universal, what's up motion. "W'sup."

I returned the gesture. "What's up."

He took me in, then nodded to the white van. "You can whip that?"

I looked back at it. Having never driven anything bigger than a car before. I was unsure, but if it meant getting Jayla back then, damn right. I faced him. "Sho 'nuff."

Reaching his pocket, he pulled out some keys and tossed em' to me. "Let's ride."

I caught em' and made my way to the driver's side of the van.

"Follow us to the spot, Tay."

"Bet." Tay went back to the car, and Redd went to the passenger side of the van.

We got in; I looked in the side mirror and adjusted the rearview. The back of the van had no seats, was junky, and I could barely see anything out the back window.

"Once you go to drivin' and bendin' them corners, that stuff back there gone be movin' around. I'm tellin' you now so you don't get nervous."

"Fasho." I crunk up the van, put my foot on the break, and pulled the gear shift down from Park, attempting to move it to Drive but it got stuck. I yanked on it twice and on the third time it gave and shifted into Drive.

I looked to Redd who wore a look of skepticism.

"You sure you know what you doin'?"

"Most definitely." I pulled off from the curb into the driveway, backed out, cutting the wheel left, and drove to the stop sign at the end of the street, after which Redd seemed to relax a little more. Not that he ever seemed tense. He appeared calm the whole time, just as he'd been the last time I saw him.

He had this chill demeanor, but everything about him

seemed calculated. I could see a lot of people being intimidated by his presence, and I decided right then that I wouldn't be one of them. I was Tonya's son and Jayla's big brother. Besides, Christmas was right 'round the corner. I wasn't about to let nobody put the boo game on me. I did need to focus, though. I didn't know what was in the back of this van that we were taking on a twenty thousand dollar move, but I didn't wanna get caught with it. I sat up. Cars were riding by into the night, but it began to lighten up. Tay pulled up behind us, and when the last car rode by, leaving a huge gap in the road before the next incoming SUV, I bussed a right into traffic.

We rode in silence for a while, and I was sure to keep both hands on the wheel. I kept glancing in the rearview mirror to make sure Tay was still behind us, only to remember I couldn't see out of it. So, I'd glanced at the side mirror instead. Over and over, I repeated this, and from the outside looking in, I couldn't help but feel like I was looking nervous. I shot a glance at Redd to see if he was watching me, and he wasn't. Too distracted, he picked something out of his pinky nail with his thumb.

He looked up straight at the road ahead, squinted and pointed. "Make this upcoming right onto the highway."

"Say no more."

The three cars ahead of me veered right one by one, and I slowly turned the wheel and followed suit. Traffic was light; all there was to see was road signs and glowing red tail lights in the night. The thick silence in the van's cab made me look to the radio but there was none. Nothing but an empty rectangle out from which a bunch of wires dangled.

"No radio."

"W-huh?" I did a double take and focused back on the road. He was still thumbing at that pinky nail.

"I was sayin' there's no radio." I felt him pause to stare at the side of my face. "That's what you were lookin' for, right? The radio?"

He was good at watching people without watching people. "Yea, fasho"

"Silence makes you uncomfortable?"

"Not really. I just figured if we gon' ride, let's ride out. Cut that shit up. Shiiid." I shrugged, looked his way, then back at the road. "Feel me?!"

He had a cocky smirk on his face. "Fasho." Sitting back, he pushed his dreads out his face and stared out his window as an 18-wheeler passed by to our right. "Tay, tell you what I said?"

"About you having to kill me if you told me the move and I wasn't with it? Yeah, he told me."

He was looking at me again. "And you wanna know?"

"Man, honestly, brah.... man, I ain't got nothin' to lose right now. I'm all in with whatever. However, this shit may come."

"Sounds like you need that bread." Redd sat back. "Care to share why?"

I went silent for a moment, debating whether or not I should but I didn't see how it could hurt at this point. "My lil sister, we all we got. Moms dead, never knew my dad, and her dad's serving life."

"Damn." Redd pointed to the lane to our right. "Get over here."

I flicked the blinker and got over.

"It'll be hard to get over here when it's time to get off at the exit, so just ride this lane."

"Fasho." I checked my side mirror to see if Tay had also changed lanes. He had, and was now two cars behind us.

"My father always said a man that grinds with a purpose doesn't just move mountains; he shapes them. Said grindin' without purpose is like sailing without a compass. You may move, but you won't reach your destination. That says a lot about you. But it doesn't say why you're willing to do anything to get this paper."

"I'm not."

"But you just said—"

"I'm willing to do anything to keep me and my sister together. That I am. The money happens to be a byproduct of that."

Redd nodded. "So, you need a lawyer?"

"Yeah. My sister's dad signed his rights over to his sister. She has her now, but I promised my sister it wouldn't be long. I want to have her back by Christmas but even with a lawyer, the chances of that happening are slim to none."

"You never know."

I looked at Redd, but he was no longer looking at me and was once again staring out his window. Not long thereafter, the city lights began to light up the sky as we approached downtown Atlanta.

I got off on I-20 Westbound Exit 58A, downtown, and made a right onto Capitol Avenue. Where Redd pointed, I turned, and this went on for twenty minutes, I was getting impatient. Not because how long it was taking to reach our destination but because we seemed to be going in circles. Passing Georgia State University for the third time I was just about to say something about it when Redd nodded slightly to the right.

"This the street right here," he said.

I flicked the right blinker and made the turn onto the narrow street. To our left was a multi-floor parking garage, and to our right was the curb and a tall, steel black gate. Pulling into the street just enough to give Tay room to park behind me I began to slow to a stop, but

Redd told me to keep going. I pressed forward. The street was short and ended at a cul-de-sac that stopped at a loft. I made a slow U-turn and drove back towards the street's entrance.

"Park right here," Redd said, pointing at the curb that was now to our left.

I slowed to a stop curbside, and Tay followed suit directly behind us. Putting the car in park, I cut the engine. Redd pulled out his phone and began texting someone while I sat, patiently waiting for whatever was coming next. Whatever it was, it didn't seem ominous enough to want to kill someone over. I glanced in my rearview mirror long enough to see Tay get out the driver side of his car and close the door behind him.

"Showtime." Redd closed his flip phone, put it in his pocket and opened the van door. "Let's do it, Lo."

Redd hopped out and I got out the van and closed the driver side door. Redd was making his way to Tay, who was standing at the head of his car. I blew my breath in my hands and rubbed them together. The night was chilly enough that I could see Tay and Redd's breath exit their nose and mouth every time they exhaled. I reached them and Redd was the first to speak.

"Yall cut yall phones off?"

Tay whipped out his phone and flashed a black screen. "You know it."

They both looked at me, and I reached in my pocket to

pull out my phone. I hit the power button on the side to cut it off, just as a text from Jayla came through.

JAYLA: I miss you...

I stared at it for a moment.

"You good?" Redd said.

"Yea." I powered the phone off releasing a heavy sigh. "Yea, I'm good." Putting the phone in my pocket, I cleared my throat. "Phone off. W'sup?"

"Shiiid, let's go." Redd turned and began walking towards the loft and we were right behind him.

We got to the loft and went to the side of where there was nothing but a huge AC unit, some bushes, a black steel gate, and a granite wall. Effortlessly, Redd maneuvered his way up the gate, shimmied across the tall stone all with his toes and fingertips, jumped up to the ledge, and pulled himself up. Tay and I stood, looking in disbelief.

Redd stood at the edge, looking down on us, waving us up. "W'sup? What yall doin'? Come on!"

Tay and I looked at each other and he went for it climbing first on top of the AC unit and attempting to climb the wall from bottom to top, before falling and starting with the gate how Redd did.

Taking a deep breath and exhaling I made my way to the gate. I looked behind me to make sure the coast was clear and seeing no one, I put my focus back on the gate.

"Here I come Jayla."

I maneuvered my way up the gate, shimmied across the

tall stone wall with my toes and fingers, jumped up to the ledge, and pulled myself up, only not as effortlessly. I stood, struggling to catch my breath.

"What?" Redd said clearly unaffected.

Tay was brushing dirt and dust off his jeans.

"Nothing." I shrugged it off. "W'sup?"

"Follow me. I'll show you." Redd walked around the side of the loft and we followed him to the front which was level with a main street. "You see this here?" He pointed to a half circle shaped window above the front door. "You're tall. Stand and look through here while we go through the back. Let us know if you see any movement."

"Aiight." I shot Tay a look as him and Redd walked off and he shrugged. I made a mental note halla at him bout this shit later. I was nobody's lookout boy. The fuck?!

I looked for something I could stand on to be able to peak through the window above the door and saw nothing in sight. I looked back at the street that was surprisingly not very busy. Even still, it was enough to get me caught if the police just so happen to stroll by. There was a tall bush just to the right of the doorstep that would block me if I stayed all the way to that side. I looked around again for something to boost me up high enough for me to look through the window and found nothing. I jumped up catching a glimpse of the inside. I jumped up again for another look at what was clearly the living room.

I jumped again and this time I saw the beam of a flashlight coming from a back window. It was straight ahead from the door, through the living room in what was obviously the kitchen. I jumped again and this time I grabbed the edge of the window and put the tip of my toe on the door hinge to hold myself up. I'd be lying like a mufucka if I said this shit wasn't uncomfortable, but I had to do what I had to do. I looked around the flashlight beam, dimly lit living room and peeped a hallway entrance to the right, just as the faint sound of breaking glass reached my ear.

It had been barely noticeable that had I not been in on what was going on I may not have known what the sound was.

I looked back to the window where the flashlight was no longer being held steady, it was moving as though they were attempting to unlock the—a figure emerged from the shadows, catching my eyes. I looked to my right and a light skin guy in nothing but basketball shorts walked into the living room scratching his head, looking confused. He did a double take and froze at the sight of the flashlight coming through the window, and in a panic he ran back to a room. I jumped down immediately and ran around the side of the loft. In my mind his reaction meant one of two things: he was going for a gun, or he was calling the police. Neither one was good. I got to the window and Tay and Redd spun around with quickness.

"Bra, somebody in that mufucka. Let's dip!"

Tay's eyes got big. "You seen em?!"

"Hell yea! Come on. Let's dip!"

We took off running to the front of the loft, hopped the black gate and was still running, but—

"Aye chill!" Redd yelled discreetly.

Tay and I paused mid stride and looked back.

Redd was walking. "We good."

We started walking up the sidewalk of the road and Redd caught up to us, walking too.

"We ain't gotta run from here. It'll only make us hot. He never saw us so play it cool."

It made sense so we did just that. We played it cool all the way back to the van and car, then all the way back to where we McAfee Road...twenty bands short.

I laid in bed that night staring up at the dark ceiling in deep thought, still unable to process the nights events. Ain't no way in fuck! What the hell had just happened? And what was so important about that move that demanded killing if someone wasn't with it? Was it the person who spot we was hittin? Was it what we were actually there to take? What?! Nothing about tonight made sense. To say I was blowed was an understatement. I was pissed the fuck off, and on the low, I was scared. I hadn't cut or turned lights on in the apartment since I got back. My chest felt tight with anxiety as I thought long and hard about what I could do to hustle up the money I needed to secure a child custody lawyer so I could get Jayla back.

. . .

KNOCK. KNOCK. KNOCK.

I RELEASED A HEAVY SIGH AT THE SOUND OF SOMEONE AT THE FRONT door. They didn't know it, but they were interrupting my thoughts. This better not be D'narius bitch ass. I had a long-ass text from him when I cut my phone on as we left the scene earlier, trying to explain himself. Apparently the guys he knew from that neighborhood had given him up. Miami Phat had been the one who called him when he panicked at Tay's house the day before yesterday when he rushed out right before I came over. The call was to tell him he knew he had his camera and .380, but he missed the Russian AK-47. Then he added that he knew where D'narius stayed and was on his way over with it. The trap had been set, and he fell for it. He had hopped out on the scene to protect his mother and got caught down bad. With no chance to even clutch for his strap, he was at Miami Phat's mercy. He made his demands: all his shit back, or D'narius was dead. I still ain't feel sorry for him. He could've got us all killed. Me in his shoes, I would've taken my lick. I rolled out of bed and made my way to the front door and looked through the peephole. My face softened when I saw Traci standing on the other side.

I opened the door. "Hey." Stepping to the side, I gestured for her to enter.

"Hey, you..." She turned to face me after she stepped inside, and I closed the door behind her. "Were you sleeping?

I'm sorry, I just wanted to come by and check on you..." She said and stuck her hands in the back pockets of her jeans.

I shook my head. "Nah, I wasn't sleep." I looked around the darkened apartment. The only light source came from the light above the stove in the kitchen area. "And I'ma be aiight. Just gotta figure some shit out." I shrugged and moved to sit on the Love seat in the living room.

Traci caught me by surprise when she sat down directly next to me. She was so close that our thighs were touching. I looked up at her and met her eyes.

"I'm sure you will... I still wanted to check on you, though." She reached forward and flicked one of my dreads out of my face to get her a better look at my face in the dim lighting.

I looked away from her, considering what she said, an unfamiliar warmth spreading through my chest. I cleared my throat. "'Preciate that."

Traci let out a long breath. "Look, I don't wanna overstep and get all in your business. I know you left earlier for something important and based on what you said... it probably didn't go well."

She lifted up a little and pulled a folded up piece of paper from her back pocket.

"I love Jayla, too, and I want to help get her back in any way I can. Here," she handed me the paper. "I made a call to my old supervisor from my old job. I was an administrative clerk for a law office, and she was a lawyer. I wasn't sure what she specialized in exactly, but I called her to see if there was any way that she could help us out. She says she's familiar enough with family law to be able to point us in the right direction at least."

I unfolded the piece of paper and found the name, number, and address of whom I assumed was the lawyer lady.

"She's good people... looked out for me while I was there. You know, sista's gotta stick together, that kind of thing." She chuckled. "Anyway... I just wanted to come by and give you that. Hopefully it'll be something helpful to you."

I shook my head as I stared down at the paper, the warmth in my chest spreading. "Thank you, Traci. For real. I'll give her a call first thing in the morning." I sat up and tucked the piece of paper under the couch cushion. I would remember that it was there.

"It's nothing, really." Traci said and stood up from the couch. "I'll go ahead and get out of your hair, though." She put her hands in her back pockets again.

I stood, and slowly we walked back to the door. I was getting ready to open it for her to let her out when I looked down at her again. "Why you always so nice and willing to help me out, T?"

The light from the kitchen was shining directly onto her face, casting a golden glow to light up her pretty face. I had always found Traci to be attractive, but it was in that moment that I found myself attracted to her. Her refusing to let Tabitha and 12 take Jayla had me looking at her in a different light.

It was one thing for her to sell me food stamps and watch my little sister occasionally, but to fight for my sister and even attempt to help me get her back...that meant more to me than she would ever know.

She didn't owe me anything, and yet she was there for me...for us—something about that set every fiber of my being ablaze with the need for her.

Traci diverted her pretty eyes from mine and shrugged her shoulders, looking shy. A nervous giggle bubbled up in her chest. "I think you're a good guy... we could all use some help every once in a while."

I stepped slowly toward her, and with each step I took towards her, she took one step back until I had her backed into the wall. Her breathing hitched when I leaned in and looked her in the eyes.

"Yea?" I cupped her cheek in his hand. "We could all use some grace." My words came out as a mumble, and I swiped my thumb across her bottom lip.

She met my eyes. "Right." Her reply came out airy.

"If I didn't know any better, I'd say you have a crush on me, Traci." I joked, my hand sliding down her neck in a soft caress that made her shiver against me.

"You saying you didn't already know that?"

I leaned down and softly pressed my lips against the exposed skin of her shoulder thanks to the off-shoulder sweater she was wearing. Her skin was soft and smelled sweet. It made my dick swell even more with need. I put both of my hands on the wall beside her as I buried my face into the crook of her neck and inhaled deeply. It was something about being so close in her space that felt good to me. I could feel her body melting into me the same way that I found my body molding itself around her.

"Didn't think I was your type," I mumbled in between kisses to her neck.

Her small hands slid underneath my shirt and caused a shiver of its own to shake my spine. "Mmm." She moaned when I gently bit her earlobe.

I removed my face from her neck and looked into her eyes. For a moment, I searched them, looking for any sign of rejection or hesitance. When I didn't find any, I leaned in slowly and pressed my lips to hers. My arms circled her when I felt her body relaxing into me, and I pulled her close as the soft and sweet kiss quickly turned passionate and needy.

In what seemed like a blink of an eye, Traci and I were stumbling through the dark apartment to my bedroom, our lips and tongues locked in a heated battle. Inside my room, the clothes started coming off.

"Oop!" Traci gasped when I gently pushed her back onto my bed, expertly peeling her pants off her lower half, exposing the pair of black lacy panties that she was wearing. I licked my lips as she took her time removing her sweater from her shoulders, revealing that she was braless underneath the wool material.

Her nipples were erect, thick, and begging to be sucked on. "Goddamn," I mumbled to myself as I hovered over her, taking in her physique before meeting her eyes again. "You sure you wanna do this?" I asked, my voice low and thick with desire. I could feel the head of my dick leaking through my shorts.

Traci was cool as hell, a good friend, and had always been there for my sister as often as I needed her to be and some. As bad as I wanted her, I didn't want to force myself on her even though she had made it clear that she was interested. Crossing that line would mean that there would be no turning back. I wasn't sure if I was ready for it, but the thought of it didn't bother me either.

"Boy, stop playin' and give me that dick. You know I been feelin' you." We laughed, and she took the initiative and began pulling my white T-shirt over my head.

Traci licked her lips and ran her hands down my bare chest as I laid between her thick thighs, my hard dick pressed directly to her middle. All that separated them was the thin pair of panties she was wearing and my basketball shorts and boxers. I wasn't sure when, but at some point, she had slipped her little feet out of her UGGS and hooked her toes into the waistband of my shorts and pushed them off my ass and down my legs. My dick twitched with need at her actions. I could tell she wanted me just as badly as I wanted her.

"Ah!" Traci gasped when I took one of her engorged nipples into my mouth. My hands slid sensually down her soft sides until they met with the band of her panties and slipped them off her hips, thighs, and down her legs.

The moment I slipped her panties off, the scent of her arousal filled my nose and made my need for her heighten. The smell of her feminine parts consumed me, making me hungrily suck on her nipple while a hand drifted between us. I took two fingers and sunk them deep into Traci's center.

I wanted to see how wet she was before I dove into her.

"Oh, Terrance." Traci moaned, one hand gripping a fist full of my dreads, the other clutching the bed sheets beneath them.

"Oh shit. This pussy wet as fuck..." I mumbled more to myself before turning my head and giving the other nipple some attention.

Her skin tasted as sweet as she smelled.

The sound of Traci's sweet moans filled the air as I spent the next few minutes slowly stroking the insides of her wet walls with my fingers while I sucked on her nipples.

"I-I'm cu– " before she could finish her sentence Traci's entire body was convulsing as I brought her to an intense orgasm. She hadn't even come down from her orgasmic high, when I slowly filled her with every inch of my dick. "Oh my gawd!" She cried while I slowly stroked in and out of her wetness, catapulting her even further into bliss.

"Ugh!" I groaned in complete pleasure. Traci's pussy gripped my dick tightly, all the while gushing all over my length and soaking my balls. "I knew yo ass had some good pussy." I grunted, hooking my hands under her knees and pushing them back into her chest so I could dig into her pussy even deeper.

"Uh hun, give it to me, Terrance. Give it to me. Oh, fuck!" Traci's arms were locked tightly around my neck, tears sliding down the sides of her face from the intense pleasure I was giving her.

Nothing but our moans and groans filled the air, our chemistry and passion making the room heat up and our naked bodies sweat. Feeling my nut building up, I hurriedly pulled out of Traci and shot my load all over the outside of her pussy and her stomach.

"Whew!" I huffed, jacking my dick to make sure I got out every drop of nut from my dick. Once done, I collapsed onto my back on the bed next to Traci where we both laid there staring up at the ceiling and catching our breath.

The moment had been unexpected for us both, but neither of us were mad about it. The sex was great.

Jayla sat in between Traci and I on the porch right outside Tabitha's spot in Point South Apartments, where we'd been for the last hour. Traci ended up sleeping over last night and this morning she suggested we go see her. I spoke to Traci's ex-employers secretary and was told she would call back due to her being in court. So, I decided to call Tabitha. We got no answer, but we came anyway. She didn't trip, though. Rather she explained that I was welcome to come see Jayla anytime. She just didn't trust me to do so out of her presence. I didn't like it, but I understood my history of running off with her and appreciated her willingness to even allow my visits.

"I hate it here! I wanna go home with you and Traci."

Jayla said. "I have no friends over here, and Tabitha said next year I'll have to switch to Pointe South Elementary."

I sighed. "Not today, Jayla. I'm comin' to get you, though."

Jayla poked her lip out. "You promise?"

I glanced at Traci, who looked uncertain but supportive all the same. Looking back to Jayla I said, "I promise."

Jayla's face lit up with a smile unearthly. Hopping up with glee, she jumped on me showering my face with kisses and all three of us laughed. Some guys walked by with orange bandanas on their heads.

Jayla pulled back and looked me face to face with her eyes full of hope. "So does this mean we'll be spending Christmas together?"

Though I wasn't sure, who was I to kill that hype? Who was I to take away what may be all that's left of something for her to look forward to? No, I wouldn't be that brother.

"Of course," I said looking Jayla in her pretty brown eyes.

"Okay," she said skeptically. "Remember what you said."

I cocked my head to the side. "What's that?"

Jayla smiled. "Lying to me is lame and it won't happen again because you love me so muchy-much." She cheesed hard with her eyes closed tight.

"Mhmm. Come here." I pulled Jayla into my embrace and held her the way I used to when she was younger. "I promise, Lala."

I sat quietly in the passenger seat of Traci's silver Altima. I had to figure this shit out. Traci and I had a few ideas, but we had to put them in action. An idea that is developed and put into action is more important than an idea that exists only as an idea. Only thing is we had all these plans and no paper. Even when her ex-employer reached back out to us with the lawyer info, what could we do unless they were willing to represent us pro bono? I barely had money to fulfill Jayla's Christmas list, let alone pay a three thousand-to-five-thousand-dollar child custody lawyer retainer fee. I shook my head as we pulled up Bar Harbor Drive, pulling in just as I received a text alert. I looked at my screen.

D'narius: Bra, Miami Phat and some niggas tried to kill me last night. I been hidin' out in this bando. I waited him out for hours last night and when I tried to walk home they shot at me again. I ran back here and stayed the night. I'm just now wakin' up.

I put my phone in my pocket on that police ass nigga. I ain't give a fuck!

Traci pulled into the uphill driveway and put the car in park. "You sure you wanna stay over here?"

I nodded slowly, staring straight ahead. "Yea…I gotta make somethin' shake."

"Terrance, I know. I just—I don't want you to get desperate and do something you might regret."

Traci's eyes were burning a hole in the side of my face, as I stared straight ahead at nothing.

I looked at her. "I hear you."

Opening the door, I got out and closed it behind me. I could hear Traci backing out of the drive way as I walked up the rose wood porch steps. Skipping the knock, I opened the door and walked right in. Muffled loud music could be heard from downstairs instantly. Closing the door behind me, I made my way down the steps and opened Tay's room door to my immediate right, releasing the blaring music into the hallway: Poppin' Them Thangs by G-Unit.

My face screwed up. "Maaan, if you don't cut this shit off!"

Tay was at his cherry wood dresser baggin' up weed. He saw me and went in. "Nigga! Don't bring that bitch ass nigga D'narius over here again!"

I was looking at the iPod. "Who the fuck downloaded a G-Unit collaboration album?"

Tay snatched the iPod from me. "Man, fuck all that! Okay, me. I did. I fuck wit' Fifty. Who I don't fuck wit' is ya boy D'narius. Bitch ass nigga been textin' me all night hidin' in a bando from the nigga who house y'all hit!"

"Bra, stop sayin' that."

"What? Y'all did! And now y'all got me in that bullshit."

"Man, you ain't got nothing to do with that."

"Shittin' me! Who's to say he won't spin the block. Especially after you was talkin' crazy. That shit he said before he left was like a warning. Now, he shootin' at D'narius! That fuck nigga ain't playin'. Whoever he is!"

"Aye, man fuck all that. I ain't worried bout him. I gotta get my sister back."

Tay ran his hand down his face. "Yeen gotta be worried bout him. He don't know where you live. He think you live here...where my mama, sister and her kids lay their head!"

Damn...it hit me like a flash mob in a quiet square. Tay was right. He had everything to lose if Miami Phat decided to do something stupid.

"You right, Bra. My bad. We done messed around and got you involved in some shit that ain't have nothin' to do with you." I sat down on the edge of his bed, elbows on my knees, and put my face in my hands. I looked up. "We can handle that nigga first. I know where he stay, too."

Tay waved it off. "Yea...but, nah. I'ma just hope for the best and expect the worse." Tay lifted his shirt to show the handle of the 9mm sticking out his waistline. "I'm on point."

"Say no more." I nodded. "What the fuck was that last night, though?"

Tay looked lost. "What you mean?"

"That move with Redd. That was the most bogus move ever. All that fake ominous shit just to take a nigga on a blank trip? Come on, Tay."

Tay stood there looking at me with a blank face.

I shifted my stance, exasperated. "Yo! The fuck wrong wit' you?"

"Nah!" Tay shook his head, reached in his pocket, and pulled out his phone. "It's crazy. He said you would pull up on me today and question me bout him and the move."

"What...when?"

Tay was texting. "Last night he called me right after we all parted ways. Said you would do exactly what you're standing here before me now doing, and when you do, I'm supposed to text him right away."

"You textin' him?" I was staring at the phone in his hand trying my damnest to read the screen.

Tay finished. "Yea. I don't think that was the move he was talkin' bout, between you and me. He was so sure you would pull up today complainin' about him and the move. Even said you would be talkin' shit. Told me to text him and he would text me an address."

His phone chimed, and he looked down at the screen. He was staring down at the screen a little too long for me.

"What?" I said.

Tay looked up and held the phone up for me to read the open text message thread on the screen.

Redd: The money is still good. The offer is still on the table with the same stipulations. If you're interested, have Tay drop you off at the address below.

Tay slowed the Dodge Magnum to a stop in front of a house on White City Road.

"This it?" I eyed the house skeptically.

"Yea, fasho." Tay cut the engine and put the car in park. I wasn't skeptical about Redd actually living here. I was more skeptical about anyone living on this street having twenty thousand dollars, let alone twenty thousand dollars to just give away. Much like the quality of my grandmother's house, it wasn't run down. It was white and brown with a small porch, and an upstairs and downstairs. The other houses that lined the street were very much the same save for some of them were different colors and others had Christmas lights adorning them.

"Let's do it," I said opening the door just as my phone chimed, alerting me that I had a message.

"I can't go with you."

I pulled my phone out and looked at my screen. It was another message from D'narius.

D'narius: I know you mad at me, bra, but be careful. In the car leaving from over there that day he said (and these are his exact words) "I don't like that light skin nigga. He talk too much." Not much from an average person, but this guy is a fuckin maniac. Be on point.

I sucked my teeth, cut my phone off, slid it in my pocket and looked back at Tay just as I was about to hop out. "What?"

"I called before we left. Bra said you gotta enter solo. Told me not to wait for you, either."

I looked to the house, then back at Tay. "What the fuck this nigga got goin' on?"

"I wish I knew." Tay shrugged. "But bra, listen..."

Tay's lips said nothing, but his eyes communicated everything. I stared into them and nodded. I knew what I had to do. Well, not really but I knew whatever I was asked to do I had to be with it. I got out, closed the door behind me and made my way to the house. I heard Tay crank up the car and pull off as I walked up the porch steps and looked back to see a tan Honda Civic with factory rims take his place just as I reached the front door. I knocked and looked back to see a woman in the car on the phone. Assuming she was lost and calling someone for directions, I minded my business and turned my attention back to the door. I knocked again and this time the door was answered by some short, swole, bald head dark skin guy.

"Come in. Redd'll be right with you." He stepped back and allowed me to enter.

I was skeptical, and the way I eyed him communicated such. I looked past him into the well-lit house. It seemed eerily quiet.

"You finna blow it already. Step in before the bitch gets out the car. She's watchin' you."

I started to look back.

"Don't look back at her, foo! Come in!" Baldy yelled in a hushed whisper.

I stepped in and closed the door behind me. "Where's Redd?"

Baldy smiled, pulled out a black and chrome .40 and pointed it at me.

I tensed up apprehensively. "What part of the game is this?"

Baldy laughed. "Watch."

"What?" My brows creased in confusion.

He waved the gun as if to gesture behind me. "Watch."

I was hesitant about turning around, thinking he would shoot me in the back of my head, but reluctantly, I looked. There was a long, slim, vertical glass window beside the door behind a curtain. I looked back at Baldy, stepped closer to the window, and peeked out the blinds. The woman who had just pulled up was walking up the small porch steps. Just as she was about to knock, five figures, who had apparently been ducked off on each side of the house, ran up behind her and drew down on her with guns. Their faces were covered with black bandannas and over their heads, they wore hoodies. Their attire was blacked out as well. She started to scream, but one of the figures put her in a headlock and it came out a choked cry. They put a chrome Glock to her head.

"Open the door," Baldy said behind me.

I opened the door, and they rushed in.

"Close it!" Baldy yelled.

I closed the door and stepped back.

Baldy approached the girl and leaned close to face. "Where the keys?"

She attempted to speak, but it came out a strained gurgle.

Baldy tapped the arm of the person who had her in a chokehold. "Loosen up. Let's hear what this rat bitch has to say."

They loosened their grip and the girl gasped for breath and began coughing.

Baldy grabbed her face. "I'm listening."

"Please don't hurt me," she said.

"Where the fuck them keys at?!"

"I-I-I, I left them in the car in the ignition. Redd said—"

"Shhhhh..." Baldy put his index finger to her lip to silence her. Pulling his hand away from her lips, he slowly stepped back. "Redd."

Instantly, one of the hooded figures standing in the rear of them all, whipped out a black-on-black Glock, and shot the one holding the girl in the head. Blood splattered on her face and she screamed as they fell to the floor. Before anyone could react, he shot the remaining three hooded figures in the head, each one of them crumbling to the floor with their heads leaking.

I was stuck. What the fuck had just happened? The woman was still screaming.

"Shut the fuck up!" The hooded figure kicked her in the face, and she fell back into a silent whimper.

Baldy looked at the dead black-on-black wearing accomplices. "A bunch of fuckin' weenies. All of em!" Baldy looked over to me. "What you see here…" He gestured towards the bloody floor, the whimpering woman and four dead bodies. "…was a big elephant size problem. Not anymore."

The hooded figure removed his hood, and it was none other than Redd. He shook his dreads out and tucked the Glock back in his waistline.

He suddenly looked at me. There was a heavy silence in the room, broken only by the woman's whimpering. "Polo," he said, his voice a low and menacing growl.

I swallowed hard, the taste of bile at the back of my throat. I glanced at the woman on the ground, her eyes wide and terror-stricken. She was sobbing now, her body trembling violently. The look in her eyes was one of desperation, a silent plea for mercy.

"Finish it," Redd commanded.

I froze for a moment, my mind racing. But I knew what I had to do. I had already told Redd I was down for whatever. I had already crossed that line. And now, there was no turning back.

Baldy held out his strap for me, and I reached out and touched it and we locked eyes. "There's only one way to eat an elephant." He smiled. "One bite at a time."

I nodded, and grabbed the strap out his hand, my hand shaking slightly as I stepped towards the woman. She tried to crawl away, but Baldy grabbed her by the hair, pulling her back.

"Please," she begged, her voice a choked whisper. "Please, don't."

I stared down at her, my heart pounding in my chest. I had never killed anyone, but for Jayla, I would. My mind was made up. For a moment, our eyes locked, and I saw a flicker of hope in hers. But it disappeared just as quickly as it had come when I pulled the trigger.

BWA!

The sound echoed in the room, followed by an eerie silence. Her body jerked once, then fell limp. Moments passed as we stared at her lifeless body, and dark crimson blood began to pool around her.

"Now that our elephant has been eaten whole, let's eat

yours." Baldy pulled out his phone and dialed a number. Putting it on speakerphone, he let it ring until someone answered. "Pokerface," he said, his voice calm and steady. "Yall handled that business."

There was a pause, then the sound of a man's voice came through the speaker.

"Fuckin' right, Bear. We got this pussy ass nigga, right here." the man responded. "He finna deliver that message to his sister, right now, if it's a go."

Bear, which was apparently Baldy's actual name, looked at me and smiled. "It's a go."

"Bet. Hold on." I could hear Pokerface movin' around in the background. Then he was talkin' to people in the background. "Say, woah. Sit his ass up...aye, nigga. Remember what we talked about? It's time to make that call."

There was some ruffling and shuffling as though they were jumping the man, until he hollered out and pleaded for his life.

"Come on, man. I said I was gon' call her. Y'all got a nigga tied up on some fuck shit. I don't een know what the fuck goin' on!"

"Shut the fuck up! Mob shit!" I heard someone else yell in the background, followed by a thump and a grunt. "Lift yo fuckin' head up. We dialin' the number now. If you don't make it happen that's on GF you getting' stabbed up in this bitch and I promise you won't make it. Then her and her husband next."

I heard a number being dialed in the background, then it was ringing on speaker phone. An older familiar sounding woman answered, and I listened as the man, voice trembling with fear, relayed the message to a Tabitha to send Jayla back to live with Terrance immediately, and in that moment I realized who he was. Jayla's father. This couldn't be real. Was I dreaming? That meant whoever Pokerface was, he was in prison. And whoever Bear was, he had enough pull to get you touched behind the wall. How could he even know who Jayla's dad was? I was beyond shocked. I was numb. Who the fuck was this nigga? I listened on as Jayla's father demanded that Tabitha relinquish custody of Jayla to me. If she didn't, they would all die. Him, her and her husband.

"Listen to me. These guys ain't playin', Tabitha. Don't call no cops, don't do nothin' stupid. Jayla's in no danger. Just send her back to Terrance. She'll be in good hands. Trust me."

It took some convincing, but she relented. I couldn't believe my fuckin' ears. Jayla was coming home.

Bear ended the call, and Redd turned to me. His eyes were cold, and there was a strange smile on his face. "Welcome to the family, Polo. You just stepped into a much bigger game. We got a lot of business to handle, but first thing's first." He gestured to the bodies. "These gotta disappear. And this house? It's gotta go up in flames. That woman's car is yours. You find your own way home."

I looked at the bodies, then at Redd and Bear. "How did you—"

"Easy. You told Redd you had a problem and what that problem was. It was nothing to find out who yo sister was, or who her father was, either." Bear smirked. "As you can see, it was also nothing to figure out where he was. We have our ways."

I wiped his gun off with my shirt and attempted to hand it to him with it laying atop of the bottom of my shirt in my hand. "Fasho."

He waved it off. "Oh, no. None of that...that's you. Keep it. Now, that woman you just offed? She was the only thing standing in the way of Kush's freedom. I'm sure you've heard of her."

My gaze shifted to Redd, then back. "I have."

"Right. As I was saying, she had her chance to drop the charges; several chances, but she didn't. Now, Kush will be up out that mufucka in no time. Free to join the team."

I nodded, understanding the gravity of what I had just done. I had just played my part in a grander scheme, a game of chess where lives were the pawns. I wasn't just Polo anymore. I was part of something much bigger now. I was part of their family. And there was no way out.

Bear snapped his fingers. "Oh, and before I forget. Redd?"

Redd reached in his pockets, pulled out two stacks of money, and handed it to me.

"That's twenty bands," Bear said as he and Redd made

their way to the door. "Enjoy ya holidays with ya sis, Fam. Better days are comin' soon. Bee-lee dat!"

Bear and Redd made their exit, and with that, I turned my attention to the grim task at hand. I had bodies to dispose of a house to burn down, and a long drive home in a dead woman's car.

CHAPTER 15

I was walking along the trail around the lake in Lake Ridge on my way to Tay' crib on Bae Harbor. I had just finished disposing of the bodies in the woods. I had wrapped the bodies, put them in the trunk of the woman's car and had been on my way to the Home Depot on highway 85 to buy a shovel, when I noticed a new one on the backseat beside a red metal galvanized can of gasoline It looked brand new, but I wasn't sure. Then I found a receipt on the seat for it, and that fucked me up. They had sent her to the store to purchase the very shovel that would be used to bury her.

I road to Riverdale trailer park, cruised to the back of the neighborhood. I unloaded the bodies and drug them to the center of the woods one by one, where I buried them forever.

Afterwards, I went back to the car, wiped it down, drenched it in gasoline and set it on fire.

Now, I was taking the long way back to Tay's house on foot. I was drained. I was coming up between two houses when I noticed an unusual white car that the bottom of Bar Harbor, posted in wait. There was exhaust fumes coming out the tail pipe. I flattened myself against the house and inched closer to get a better view. I was a Chevy Malibu! That was Miami Phat!

I didn't have the clearest view, but I could see that there were two people in the car, one driver and one passenger. They were laying on me at the bottom of the hill!

Instantly, my hand went to my waistline to retrieve the pistol Bear had just given me. It was a cold dead night, and I was about to let these fuck niggas have it. Making sure it wasn't on safety, I ran up on the car and emptied the clip in the front part of the car, their passengers bodies jerking with each shot I fired until there was nothing left.

The air was cold, and the night was dead quiet save for the barking dogs. Business handled; I took off towards the lake once again. Tay's house was now definitely out of the question. I started to send a text to him, letting him know what was going on but I decided against it know that I had probably caught a body. I hit a cut and came out in a neighborhood inside Lake Ridge called West shore, deciding to call Traci instead.

She answered on the third ring, sounding like she was just dead sleep. "Terrance?"

"Wake up. I need you to come get me. I'm in trouble."

There was shuffling in the background instantly. I could tell she was getting up and getting ready. "Where are you?"

"I'ma be at the Shell gas station on 138. The closest one to the daycare by Lake Ridge."

"Are you okay?"

"Yea, I'm cool. I just need you to come get me. RICH'SAP!"

"I'm on my way. Leaving out now."

We hung up and I slowed to a walk, making sure to stay off the main street and close to the shadows that the house provided all the way to the gas station.

Catching my first body tonight had made me realize one thing: I could do it again if I needed to.

The following morning Traci and I went shopping crazy. I got Jayla everything on her list and some. Traci was beyond happy to put me on game about all the girl clothes and trends for Jayla, and I was thankful because I would've been so lost had she not. We were in the middle of Southlake Mall, having just left out of *Champs* shoe store grabbing Jayla's Air Maxes and to show my appreciation, I told her to pick some things out for herself, too, but she declined. I insisted, but she was adamant about not taking anything from me. I told her it was okay. Let her know that we no longer needed money for a lawyer, and that we were picking Jayla up from her Tabitha's spot after we ducked off all of Jayla's Christmas stuff at her place.

"Like, she's gonna let you get her? Just like that, no questions?" A white man and woman walked by with their two kids, eating big pretzels. All around us the mall was alive, and from where we stood we could smell the food court.

"Yep."

Traci was brow creased in confusion, as she looked me up and down. Her eyes shifted to all the stuff we had for Jayla so far that just yesterday I couldn't afford, then came back to me. "If I asked you what was going on, would you even tell me?"

I looked her in her eyes. "I would."

"Everything?" Her eyes narrowed.

"Everything." I didn't so much as blink.

Traci took a deep breath and released a heavy sigh. "Do I even wanna know?"

I shrugged. "Probably not."

She nodded, seemingly contemplating the small exchange we had just had. "Then I won't ask."

It was my turn to be surprised. I wasn't expecting that at all. True she hadn't asked me what happened last night when I got in the car; even after seeing that my clothes were covered in dirt and blood.

"You sure?"

"Positive. I want you and everything that comes with you, Terrance. Whatever it is just know I got you. I'm with you, and I'm here for you."

"Fasho."

We stopped at Walmart, and I had her go in and buy me

some bullets for the gun I got from Bear the night before. Karma was real, I had 3 bodies under my belt, and lackin' was something I was not doing.

Hours later we pulled up in Pointe South Apartments, whipping the car around to the back. It was one of the winter days where the sun was high in the sky with no clouds, but it still managed to be cold as fuck. Call me paranoid, but I was debating on whether I should show up or not.

"Aye, yo, stop the car."

Traci eased the car to a stop a little pass the office. "What?"

I just sat quietly, staring straight ahead. I had never contacted her. She didn't know about the bodies. What did I have to lose?

"Everything alright?"

I nodded.

"You sure?"

"Yea, I'm good." I nodded again. "You can go."

She stared at me a while longer but continued on in silence. Moments later we arrived. Not bothering to pull into a space, we just pulled in front of Tabitha's apartment building and honked the horn twice. I got out the car, just as Tabitha's front door opened and Jayla came running out all excited and giddy.

"You came back for me!" She gave me the biggest hug ever, and in that moment...in our little slice of time...everything was okay.

I squeezed her tight like she would disappear if I let her go. "I always come for you. I promise." I released her and pulled back. "Where's all your stuff?"

"In the living room. Aunt Tabitha told me to pack everything this morning cause I was going back to live with you."

"Go get it."

"Okay." Jayla ran to go get her things, and my eyes followed her to the door, where Tabitha stood watching me from the door frame. Her eyes were a mixture of fear and disappointment. I wanted so badly to explain that I had nothing to do with what happened to her brother, but at the end of the day, I did. Besides...I doubted she would believe me, either way. No sense wasting my breath. All I wanted them to understand was to not play with me bout my sister.

We held each other's gaze, Tabitha and I until Jayla returned with her bags. I grabbed it from her and threw it in the trunk while she went and hopped in the backseat. Closing the trunk, I made my way back to the passenger side and climbed in, slamming the door behind me. I looked out the window at Tabitha, and we locked eyes again, and they stayed lock...until finally, Traci pulled off.

Jayla was already awake when I walked into the living room, the Christmas tree lights reflecting off her wide eyes. Traci was seated on the couch, sipping her coffee, and watching as Jayla sorted through the presents under the tree. Our home was now her home, she was the missing piece that made our family whole.

"Merry Christmas, Terrance," Traci said, her eyes meeting mine. She gave me a knowing smile, one that conveyed the depth of our shared experiences and secrets.

"Merry Christmas, Traci." I said, moving to sit next to her on the couch. The warmth of the room was comforting, the scent of pine and cinnamon filling the air.

Jayla turned around, her eyes shining. "Terrance, can I

open the presents now?" She asked, her voice filled with excitement.

I chuckled. "Go ahead, Jayla. It's Christmas."

She squealed and dived into the presents, tearing the wrapping paper with a kind of childish enthusiasm that I hadn't seen in a long time. As I watched her, I couldn't help but think about how close I had come to losing her, to losing all of this.

Traci leaned against me, her head on my shoulder. "We almost didn't have this, Terrance." She said quietly. "We were so close to losing everything."

I nodded. "I know. But we didn't. We're here, we're a family. We stick together, no matter what."

Traci looked up at me, her eyes filled with a mixture of love and worry. "And we always will be, right? Together, I mean."

I wrapped my arm around her, pulling her closer. "Always and forever, Traci."

Jayla looked up from her presents, her face bright with joy. "I'm glad we're all together. I love you, Polo. I love you, Traci."

"We love you too, Jayla," Traci replied, her voice choked with emotion.

I watched as Jayla turned back to her presents, her laughter filling the room. It was a perfect moment, one that I wished could last forever. But I knew it couldn't. I knew there were strings attached to this peace, to this happiness. I had made deals, crossed lines that I could never uncross.

As I watched Jayla laugh and Traci smile, I felt a pang of guilt. I knew that the world outside was not as simple, not as pure as this moment. But for now, I pushed those thoughts aside. Today was Christmas, and I was here with the people I loved most in the world. I was grateful for that, for them. And I would do whatever it took to keep them safe, to keep us together.

But as the laughter filled the room, I couldn't help but remember the words of Redd. "Welcome to the family, Polo. You just stepped into a much bigger game."

And I knew, deep down, that the game was far from over.

Did you enjoy the read?
Let us know how much by leaving us a review on Amazon and Goodreads.

HAPPY HOLIDAYS
FROM ELIJAH R. FREEMAN & URBAN AINT DEAD.

PREVIEW

Keep reading for a preview of...

The Hottest Summer Ever

By Elijah R. Freeman

PROLOGUE

RELUCTANT

Lighting flashed, thunder boomed and heavy rain pelted the top of the stolen Toyota Corolla as I made my way home. Feeling like time was working against me, I pushed the car past the speed limit, throwing caution to the wind. I was in a lot of pain. The adrenaline rush from my mission had subsided and the wear and tear on my shoulder was catching up to me. There was no time to acknowledge pain though. More imperative issues were on my mind. Like why Keisha hadn't told us about the unexpected visit that caused her not to eradicate all traces left by the crew. We could have done damage control before things had gotten this far.

Everyone was dead now. No wonder Keisha had backed

out of the streets to go legit. She was running from her past. Her karma. Yet it found her. Her, Redd and Polo; and there was still a loose end unattended. A loose end with all the answers to my remaining questions but would create new problems. Seeing who I'd just seen moments ago reminded me just how small the world really was. It also reiterated the fact that anything was possible and to always expect the unexpected. That along with my knowledge of Zoepound and the little I remember of what Keisha disclosed about them confirmed my suspicions and broke my heart at the same time. Redd was right.

I pulled into the driveway and sat there, trying to fix myself up in an attempt to stop the pain, physical and emotional. It was 4 am. I didn't want to do it but I grabbed my strap. My life was damaged beyond repair. Chelsea was the single thread that held it together. Without her, my whole world would fall apart. What was the point in having money if there was no one to share it with? No one from the bottom to look back with from the top. I'd spend the rest of my life in question. Wondering if the people around me loved me for me, or simply for what I could do for them. That's no way for a woman to live. A lot could've been different, and staring at the gun in my hands, all the mistakes I made throughout life came rushing back...

CHAPTER 1

CRUSHED DREAMS

Born and raised in College Park, it's no surprise that I turned out to be a product of my environment. I was born to Richard and Nicole Love on March 28th, 1990 at Grady Memorial, one of Georgia's prominent hospitals. At the last minute before signing my birth certificate they decided on a name, Richelle Kemoni Love. Then a few days after I was pronounced healthy, my mother was discharged and they were finally able to take me home to our small apartment on Godby Road.

I was daddy's little girl. Whatever I wanted, I got. I loved my mama, but me and daddy just always had a deeper relationship. Daddy felt children were smarter than what a lot of people gave them credit for. As a result, he spoke to me as if I was a lot older than I actually was. I was always with him, even when he would stop by some of his stash houses. He never sheltered me from what was going on, and because of this, I grew up more advanced than most kids in my neighborhood. For me, there was no Santa Clause, Easter bunny or Prince Charming. It was just daddy, my knight in shining armor. He was my everything. His every movement was geared towards providing for me and mama, and to give me the life he never had. For a while he did. My daddy, my uncle Ron, and their childhood friend, Big Rod had found a plug and was on the come up. Then one night everything changed.

I was nine when my daddy was killed. He was just starting to make a name for himself in the dope trade. The competition felt the need to get rid of him. It was the summer of '99. I was awakened from my sleep by a loud commotion. Daddy always told me never to come looking if I sensed trouble in the house. I didn't. I went to hide instead, lying flat on my back in the bathtub. Moments later there were gunshots. I closed my eyes and prayed to the heavens.

It was another thirty minutes before I left the tub and tip-toed down the stairs, peeking around corners. Whoever it had been was long gone. I made my way over to the living room, tears came streaming from my eyes. I was young but I lived in the hood and was no stranger to gunshot wounds. I picked up the phone, dialed 911, and told them my daddy had been shot. I ran over to see if he was okay. I was crying profusely. I could barely see when I knelt down beside him. "Never forget everything I taught you." Those were his last words.

"I love you, daddy. Don't leave me."

He smiled... and that was that.

When mama and the police finally arrived, daddy was long gone. Responses to calls for help from Godby were always slow.

Daddy never kept work in the house, but he was a known drug dealer. The authorities wrote his death off as drug-related. They didn't care. He was just one less nigga they had to worry about. Mama and I moved into an apartment in Red Oak Projects that daddy had in case of an emergency. Big Rod would check up on us from time to time, but my uncle disappeared. No one told me where he went, and when I asked, they acted like it was a secret or something. Big Rod took me to get ice cream often after my daddy died. Every Friday I would wait anxiously in the window for him to show up in his money green El Dorado. He would get out standing tall, big and black, putting you in the mind of Bruce-Bruce. I was always happy to see him and ran out the door to greet him, jumping up and down knowing that I was about to receive something to my childish delight. Mama liked it, too. It gave her a break.

Big Rod would lift me up, spin me around and put me in the front seat. It was on one of these days while waiting in line for ice cream at a Dairy Queens in Riverdale that some tall, bald, dark skin guy wearing blue jeans, all white soulja Reebox and a Lakers Jersey approached Big Rod and asked about my uncle.

"Heard anything from ya boy Ron?"

Big Rod shook his head. "No, and you won't either. Nobody has. I'm starting to think he's dead."

"That would be best for him," the man scoffed. He started to walk off but noticed me, and paused.

I turned to look up at Big Rod, who stared back at the man expressionless. I looked back at the man, he looked up at Big Rod and shook his head.

"That's crazy," he said.

Without another word, he walked away. Five minutes later, we got our ice cream, left, and headed to Riverdale Park where Big Rod watched me play until the sun began to set.

Weeks turned into months and as the year went on, ice cream Fridays with Big Rod became less frequent, and before I knew it, he stopped showing up altogether. That's when things changed and I began to feel the weight of my reality.

Mama was one of the baddest bitches in the hood until she started fucking with that shit. And yes, I do mean crack. She had a bitch ass boyfriend named Darrel who was always watching me. At ten years old, I was ignorant of the lust in his eyes and he eventually violated me. I had just come home from school and mama wasn't there, so that bastard had his way with me. She must have been chasing the best high of her life because she didn't return for hours.

Darrel was sitting on the sofa watching *Leprechaun In The Hood* when he saw me. "Hey baby."

"What the fuck? I'm not your baby," I said.

I went to my room to change clothes. I could feel the vibe of someone watching me. I turned around to find it was Darrel's nasty ass. These mere events along with the fact that he used to beat my mama were the reasons I was filled with distaste and rage when it came to him. "Get away from my door!" I yelled.

He came in, closing the door behind him. "Making big demands for someone so little."

He reached for me. I tried to run but he slapped the shit out of me. The force from his strong hand sent me reeling to the floor. I was disoriented and seeing stars as he began removing the rest of my clothes. "Just take it and the pain will go away," he spoke through clenched teeth. I was scared and tears were abundantly rolling down my cheeks. "I've been wanting this for a long time," he said, pinning me down with a rough grunt.

I tried to fight back but he was stronger than me. Every time I tried to buck on him taking off my clothes he would slap me. Eventually, he got me naked and jammed his dick inside me. He broke my hymen and tore my insides apart. It hurt so bad. I cried and screamed the whole time. Blood was everywhere.

There are some things you can't see happening to you until they do. That was the day I stopped believing in God. I was only in the fifth grade and he'd done nothing but make my life hell. I figured I couldn't be sent to hell if I was already there. I didn't tell mama. She was too *dickmitized*. Plus, he was the one bringing in what little food we did have, if that counts for anything. Thursdays and Fridays were his days off and he wanted me to be there. On the days I wasn't, he would beat me. This went on for a while until I was more than fed up with his shit.

I awoke to him arguing with mama one morning. It escalated and I came to her defense. "Get off my mama!" I was trying to pull him away from her. I never saw his hand. I felt it, it sent me flying to the wall. My mouth was bleeding and my ears were ringing.

"Leave my baby alone!" my mama screamed from the floor of our small living room.

He stomped her and told her to shut up. That's when I ran out of the living room and came back with Darrel's .38 special. With hot, angry tears pouring down my face, I screamed at the top of my lungs for him to get off my mama. He turned and looked me in the eyes.

"Shoot me, bitch, if you got the heart."

I thought about all the shit he did to me, and I pulled the trigger twice.

BWA! BWA!

His eyes were a mixture of shock and disbelief as he hit the floor, bleeding to death. The gun fell from my trembling hands. Mama screamed like Tyra Banks in *Higher Learning*. I sat on the carpet and stared at Darrel's lifeless body. The nosy ass neighbors called the police and they took me away. I did ten months in the Metro RYDC.

Mama never came to see me, let alone claim me and I was eventually placed in a group home in the middle of Hillandale, another neighborhood in College Park with seven other girls. All of them were lame as hell, except one. Her name was Chelsea. I didn't know much about her because she never talked about her past. Still and yet, for some reason, I liked her in the type of way I should've liked boys. A lot of girls hated me because all the boys wanted me, but I wasn't even interested in them, to be honest. I was attracted to pretty girls. I dressed feminine but I had more nigga tendencies than the average girl should. I guess because of the way I grew up. At least that's what I came to believe.

Everybody had a mentor who brought them things, except me, and when they came to visit the group home, I'd be assed out every trip. For months, I used to cry myself to sleep until one day I decided something had to shake. Now in the seventh grade, niggas would try to fuck with me but I would never buy into it. I knew what niggas wanted, and it didn't turn me on. I was repulsed by the thought of a dick inside of me. Chelsea turned me on, though. We were basically joined at the hip. She turned out to be quite gorgeous. She was a redbone with a petite frame, cute face, like one of those Disney girls, with long brown hair to frame it.

Anyway, when I realized I didn't like boys, I tended to keep a lot of female company. To my surprise niggas started to hate on me, throwing salt on my name when they could. All but one, his name was Redd. He had a light brown skin tone. His dreads were to his neck and he stood about five-nine with a medium build. His grandparents were strong believers in the teachings of Marcus Garvey, and his parents were Rootical Rastafarians who believed in the holistic way of life. While they were full Jamaicans who came to the States in the '80s, Redd grew up on Gresham Road in East Atlanta. He was a Grady baby to the fullest.

His family had come to America on a banana boat, running from the Kingston authorities. Once here, they changed their last name to Hicks and started over. Arriving in the middle of the crack era, Redd's father, Jamaica Ray, learned the recipe and went to work. He put together a crew of thoroughbreds and painted the city red. At the height of his success with Jamaican novelty shops, a Caribbean Cuisine spot, and a club called Amadu's, Raphael Hicks was born. That was two years before my time.

By Redd's eleventh birthday so much attention had been

drawn to Jamaica Ray. The Feds had an ongoing investigation and eventually seized everything he owned. Jamaica Ray was arrested and extradited to Jamaica where he would never see the light of day again. Redd's mother was taken into Federal custody for several murders, conspiracy, and drug trafficking charges. Guilty with no way to escape, the woman hung herself. She was found in her cell one morning during breakfast. Redd said she was believed to have been pregnant, but he wasn't sure. It was sad.

Subsequently, Redd was adopted by a money hungry couple who didn't care how long he stayed out, what he did or who he did it with. Redd lived a lawless life. He believed that, because he was from ATL, he was above the law. He didn't take shit from nobody and his reputation made a lot of people scared of him.

Redd and I started rocking with each other. We smoked so much damn weed he started calling me Kush, and the name stuck. My girlfriends would get mad because they thought I was fucking him, but that wasn't the case. We were just cool. We even had our own secret duck off, that only we knew about, down the street from Mary McLeod Bethune Elementary. We'd meet there whenever Redd had stolen something and wanted to show off, which was often.

My first lick was with him. I was pretty fucking nervous. Not because it was my first, but because it was a dope boy named Champ. He had pull all through the city. At the age of eighteen, he had more money than most niggas his age. I mean, he wasn't Big Meech or nothing but he damn sure was plugged in. Redd didn't seem to care, so I said fuck the shit too. His spot was on the eastside and I hardly went out that way.

We went in through the window of his ground level home in Meadow Lane off Glenwood Road. We found a .380, eight hundred dollars, and some weed. Redd said it was a Quarter Pound.

Although we didn't get much, Redd let me keep the .380. That was my first strap. The money and weed were split down the middle. Four hundred was the most I ever had in my pocket. Most of my money came from females I fucked with. I had a mouthpiece for a bitch because I knew what they wanted. Chelsea would get mad when she saw me with other girls. Couldn't say I blamed her, though. I was jealous at times myself. The only difference was I never showed it. I had a reputation to keep. I could have any bitch I wanted and the ones who got no talk were green with envy.

I was jumped more times than I care to remember. I stayed getting into fights and stayed thirsty to hit licks with Redd. He just seemed to know so much. I began to see him as my only way out the hood but he saw hitting licks as his only way out. Still, we were all we had.

Available Now

On all online retail book platforms!

BOOKS BY

URBAN AINT DEAD's C.E.O

Elijah R. Freeman

Triggadale

Triggadale 2

Triggadale 3

Tales 4rm Da Dale

The Hottest Summer Ever

Murda Was The Case

Murda Was The Case 2

Murda Was The Case 3

OTHER BOOKS BY

URBAN AINT DEAD

Tales 4rm Da Dale

The Hottest Summer Ever

By **Elijah R. Freeman**

Despite The Odds

By **Juhnell Morgan**

Good Girl Gone Rogue

By **Manny Black**

Hittaz

Hittaz 2

Hittaz 3

Coldhearted

By **Lou Garden Price, Sr.**

Charge It To The Game

Charge It To The Game 2

A Summer To Remember With My Hitta

Snatched Up By A Hitta

By **Nai**

A Setup For Revenge

By **Ashley Williams**

Ridin' For You

Trickin' on a Beaux for Christmas: A BBW Love Story

By **Telia Teanna**

The State's Witness

The State's Witness 2

By **Kyiris Ashley**

Stuck In The Trenches

Stuck In The Trenches 2

By **Huff Tha Great**

The Swipe

By **Toōla**

Melted the Heart of a Menace

By P. Wise

Merry Trapmas: Ice & Frost

By **Mia Sky**

COMING SOON FROM

Despite The Odds 2

Hittin' Licks For The Holidays: Chicago

By **Juhnell Morgan**

Charge It To The Game 3

By **Nai**

The State's Witness 3

By **Kyiris Ashley**

Ridin For You, Too

Homie Hoppin' for the Holidays

By **Telia**

A Setup For Revenge 2

By **Ashley Williams**

Falling For A Texas Savage

By **Juanita TheAuthor**

A Millionaire Under The Mistletoe

By **Mia Sky**

Pretti & The Beast

By **P. Wise**

STAY CONNECTED

Follow
Elijah R. Freeman
On Social Media
FB: Elijah R. Freeman
IG: @the_future_of_urban_fiction